Book One

The Machine

Resurrection

By

Philip N. Rogone

The Machine: Resurrection

Copyright © March 2012 by Philip N. Rogone

This is a work of fiction. The names, characters, places, and incidents are the product of the author's imagination or are used fictitiously. Any resemblance to actual events, locales, or persons, living or dead, is entirely coincidental.

Cover Design by Philip N. Rogone
Edited by

ISBN

Paperback: 97809725143-2-3
Hardcover: 978-0-9864209-6-2

This book is dedicated to the lasting memory of the author

DON PENDLETON

whose visual way of writing made this young teenage boy want
to read for the first time, and as a result, it changed my life.
As Don wrote so often, Live Large.

Contents

"War is cruelty, and you cannot refine it."

General William T. Sherman

"I will become the unseen, doing the unthinkable. I will bring my horror to the foot of their door, creating an uncontrollable fear that will make the enemy too cautious and too frightened, and it's just where I want them to be."

PFC. Michael Angelino

Prologue

"Michael viene sull'arresto che gioca intorno." The Italian voice yelled from behind the delicatessen counter for his son to stop fooling around.

"Gee, Pop, I'm not." Michael lied as he quickly placed the folding knife back into the front pocket of his worn Levi jeans.

"We gotta cutta the beef." His father yelled back at him in his best broken English.

Michael got excited and ran behind the counter to put on a crisply starched white apron. He took out his personal German butcher knife from a large stainless steel drawer and rushed to the walk-in refrigeration unit. There, hanging from metal hooks, were four sides of Angus beef. He had learned years before from his father the art of butchery. So Michael wasted no time cutting one of the bloody slabs into fine steaks. While his blade sliced gracefully through the fresh beef muscle with the precision of a surgeon, Michael would name each cut of beef and the anatomical structure.

"Hindquarter, porterhouse, sirloin steaks, rump roast, stew meat, and of course some corned beef for our Irish customers. Oh, be gosh and be gora!" He finished in his best Irish brogue.

He moved on to the next slab, imagining his future.

"Doctor Angelino, surgeon extraordinaire, has just completed another amazing surgery." He envisioned accolades from the other doctors while using his blade to move gracefully from one corpse to the other.

By the time his father made it to the back walk-in, Michael was finishing with his last four-legged patient.

"Molto buon il mio figlio! Good Job, my son!" His father said enthusiastically.

"Thanks, Pop. I love the practice." Michael smiled back at his father as he washed off his butcher knife, returned it to its sheath, removed his blood-soaked apron, and threw it into the laundry bin near the walk-in refrigerator.

Michael Angelino was just under six feet tall with wavy blond hair, a million-dollar smile, and bright green eyes. He had an athletic body, mostly from his love of running. A senior in high school, Michael had lettered all four years in track and field and found himself with only two weeks left till graduation. A photographic memory gave him plenty of time to focus on his real interest, which was human anatomy and human physiology. For Michael, it wasn't enough to know what each body part was called; he wanted to know its function as well. It had long been his plan to go to college and then medical school, but money was tight for his immigrant Italian family, and the ongoing war in Viet Nam was escalating to a fevered pitch.

Michael received his lottery number for the draft. Eighteen years old and not yet registered for college meant only one thing: with the number twenty-six, the young boy's dreams would have to be placed on hold. He thought about his options, which had just become fewer.

He went down to the local Army recruiter and began asking questions regarding his possible job options if he decided to join rather than wait for his number to be called up. The recruiter told him that if he signed up for a three-year hitch, he had a better chance of getting his choice of assignments.

"Of course, if they feel they need you in another area, they will have the right to move you, but that rarely happens if you enlist for three." He said with assurance in his voice.

The recruiter shook his hand and emphasized his assumption that it was almost a guarantee he would get a military occupation specialty of medic as he requested. Michael wanted an opportunity to get started in the field of medicine, and if this was his best course of action, he was going to take it. Michael signed his enlistment papers, feeling pretty good about his decision.

Michael sat with his parents and discussed his plan. His parents were saddened by his choice, mostly out of guilt because they knew they didn't have the funds necessary to put him through college.

"You know, I just don't think I could stand sitting in a classroom for another four years." The young man lied to his parents.

Elizabeth Carter had been crying and moping around ever since she heard he received his draft status. Michael knew she wasn't going to take the news very well, so when he arrived, he asked her to sit on the front porch with him. She loved him the moment they met their freshman year, and they had been inseparable through their four years together.

Elizabeth looked deep into his beautiful emerald eyes and asked, "You're going, aren't you?"

"I signed the papers today." He said.

He proceeded to tell her that he had signed up for three years to be sure he would get medical school training to be a medic.

"If I had signed for two years, I would probably get sent to the front lines as an infantry soldier." He announced his decision proudly. This information didn't comfort her like he had hoped it would.

"They will send you right in the middle of all the fighting, Mike." She declared through her tears.

"You may be right, Elle, but I might be able to keep our soldiers alive, once they've been wounded." Elizabeth watched his face for an answer that would bring her comfort. He tried to reassure her.

"Don't worry, Elle, God will watch over me, just like he always has."

"Your faith is stronger than mine, Mike." She confessed, wiping the tears from her eyes as she stood up. Michael wanted her to understand, so he stood facing her and placed his hands on her arms.

"What would you rather have me do, run off to Canada?" Michael spoke patriotically. "This is my country. My number was pulled. I will do my duty."

He then grabbed her arms more tightly and held her firmly as he continued looking deep into her eyes, "and you'd better wait for me, cause when I get home, I'm gonna marry you. Do you understand?"

Elle stared at Michael, unable to speak. Suddenly, she began to giggle while she was crying, "Are you proposing to me?"

"I guess I am." He said as a matter of fact. She looked at him, her eyes filled with excitement, unable to muster any words.

"So what's your answer?" He questioned softly with a small grin, as he began to see the humor in his request.

"Of course I'll marry you. How could I refuse? You're so romantic." She said with great sarcasm. She threw her arms around him and gave him a long, adoring kiss.

Michael looked down at her beautiful face; his young, strong arms wrapped around her, and he said apologetically, "I'll get better at the romance part, Elle, I promise."

Two weeks after their high school graduation, Michael found himself just outside a Greyhound bus bound for Fort Dix in New Jersey. His mother was shaking as she cried, and Michael held her close.

"Mom, I'll make you proud of me." He tried to comfort her.

"I'm already proud of you, my son." She responded to him

"I'll be home before you know it." He assured her.

He turned to his father and was surprised to see tears welling up in his eyes.

"Geez, Pop, you're gonna make me fall apart here," Michael said as he hugged his father.

"Ti amo son." His father told him.

His father reached into his pocket and pulled out a solid gold crucifix, unhinged it, and put it around his son's neck.

"Wear it all the time, my son. God will protect you. I had Father Pinta bless it for you."

"Thanks, Pop, I will." He said as he put his hand on the cross.

Elle watched his parents cry and began to weep when he turned to her. She couldn't speak, so she wrapped her arms around his neck and kissed him with a passion she had never expressed to him before. They had promised to save themselves for each other and abstain from sex until they were married, but the kiss was saying so much more. His knees got a little weak.

He looked deep into her beautiful blue eyes. "I love you and only you forever, Elle."

He got on the bus and positioned himself next to the window; his family waved one more time before the bus left the station and onto the expressway. He gazed out the Greyhound window and watched as Elizabeth and his Mom sobbed in each other's arms. He thought about that last kiss from Elizabeth and the life he was leaving behind. His head filled with excitement and apprehension.

When the military transport came to a halt just inside the Fort Dix processing center, a screaming voice from outside was ordering them to get off the bus. Michael hurried off the vehicle and passed a very small dark skinned Asian soldier wearing a Smokey the Bear hat on his head, who was the voice. Michael smiled. A second later, the tiny man was in his face.

"What's so funny, mister?" The small soldier screamed.

Michael instinctively responded, "Nothing, sir."

The Drill Instructor moved nose to nose and screamed at him. "Do I look like an officer to you, maggot? I work for a living. You will address me as Drill Sergeant Ortega."

He then turned away and repeated, "You will all call me Drill Sergeant Ortega."

The entire group of young men shouted, "Yes, Drill Sergeant!"

The sergeant yelled back even louder, "I can't hear you."

During the induction process, Michael's head was shaved bald, and he was poorly outfitted in an array of olive drab clothes, green shirts, green pants, green socks, green underwear, and black combat boots. He also met young men from different regions of the country, all just as frightened as he was about what all this meant.

The next eight weeks of basic training turned out to be just the hell he thought it might be. Every morning at five, it was calisthenics. This was followed by approximately seven minutes to eat breakfast before being screamed at to move out. Inspection each day was to ensure that each soldier's area was perfectly in order. Everything had a place, and anything that wasn't where it was supposed to be meant push-ups until the soldier's arms went numb. This was usually followed by putting on complete field packs and a twenty to thirty-mile hike up and down the hills of the base. Lunch was usually only five to seven minutes long, and then it was hand-to-hand combat. They were given detailed instructions on how to kill a man as quickly as possible. Each day ended with a clean-up of the area around the barracks before being rushed to dinner. Every soldier was required to know the code of conduct, general orders while on post, and you needed to be able to recite every word if questioned. It was not too unusual to be awakened at three thirty in the morning for no reason but to be able to recite the specifications of the M-16 rifle.

Michael's appreciation for his superiors increased when he was escorted into a gas chamber. Once inside, his gas mask was removed, and an unmasked Drill Instructor, seemingly unaffected by the poisonous gas, asked him his name, hometown, social security number, and anything else he could think of until Michael was coughing uncontrollably. As he began to lose his legs from the poison, another Instructor assisted him outside. Michael was coughing with eyes so watery that he could not see. He rubbed his eyes in disbelief because the Drill Instructor was still standing in the gas chamber with no mask on and talking to each soldier in his unit. Michael began to understand the importance of not just learning what he was being taught but living it.

About halfway through their training, the recruits were instructed in the art of crawling through a barbed wire fence while live rounds were being fired just overhead. It was to teach them to move forward despite taking on fire. One of the soldiers remarked that they wouldn't use real ammunition on a training exercise, and he would prove it, so during the mock attack, the soldier stood up. The instructor's machine gun stopped firing, but not before a bullet pierced through the soldier's uniform. Michael was the closest to the soldier and crawled over to him as the drill came to an abrupt end and the field lights came up. His Drill Instructor was surprised to see Michael applying direct pressure to the wound and talking to the soldier to keep him calm. The Sergeant made a mental note of the incident. Michael began to be watched more closely as he seemed to have a real grasp on the importance of each training exercise and superior reaction skills.

Each unit was required to keep its barracks spit-shined and always ready for inspection. The worst company would be given the humiliating distinction of Eight Ball Platoon and would have to carry an Eight Ball flag during drill exercises. Michael's company carried that flag for most weeks.

His Drill Instructor, Sergeant John Harris, was a hard-looking black man who had already served two tours of duty in Viet Nam. He told them, "I don't care if you are the eight ball platoon, because it isn't going to be how clean you keep your quarters, but how clean you keep your rifle."

As a result of the drill instructors' priorities, Michael's unit scored higher than all the other units when they were out in the field. When it came to actual combat situations, their company was the best. Michael especially caught the attention of his superiors on the rifle range. Michael was so good with a rifle; his commanding officer put him in a rifle competition between all the brigades at the camp. He easily defeated the other men with perfect bull's eyes from every distance. His Commander, Colonel Pruitt, called in Michael's Drill Instructor.

"Sergeant Harris, do you think Angelino could be special operations material?" Pruitt asked.

The Sergeant replied, "Sir, Angelino is an excellent soldier, on top of being the best damn shot I've ever seen in my eighteen years of service. When Private Jones was shot during our field exercise, Angelino was on him instantly and kept direct pressure on his wound, which probably saved his life. His overall reaction time seems to be split seconds faster than anybody I have put him up against in hand-to-hand combat. He has used pressure techniques to overpower even the biggest opponents that I have never seen used. Special ops might be a great way to use all those skills."

"Set it up, Sergeant Harris. We only have a few weeks before he goes to A.I.T. Put him through the test. If he passes, we'll change his orders." Pruitt demanded.

"Yes, Sir," barked back the Drill Instructor, knowing the test would be a simple one but not found in any Army manual.

A day later, Michael entered the latrine to relieve himself during a brief break. He paid very little attention to the two unfamiliar soldiers near the row of sinks. He unzipped his fly and began to reach into his pants when he felt the movement of someone coming toward him. Reacting instinctively to potential danger, the first rushing soldier was met with a fist to the throat. He was paralyzed, reaching for his damaged neck with both hands and dropping to his knees. Michael felt a large arm wrap around his neck. As the second assailant began to squeeze tightly, Michael brought his left combat boot heel down with full force onto the soldier's toe. This gave him just enough time to slip out of the neck hold and deliver an explosive blow to the nose with such force that his enemy fell unconscious at his feet. He turned his attention back to the first man, who was still holding his damaged neck. Michael kicked him as hard as he could in the groin and watched as the misguided soldier fell forward onto his face. He looked down at the unmoving men, then casually went back to the urinal, relieved himself, washed his hands, and left.

Once outside, he was approached by an unfamiliar officer. Michael saluted. As the salute was returned, the officer spoke.

"Private Angelino, please come with me."

"Yes, sir. May I ask the Captain where we're going?" Michael responded.

The Captain answered back, "You will find out soon enough, soldier." The Captain looked at Michael and then gave him a very small grin.

"Did you have a problem in the latrine?"

"No, sir," Michael answered back. "Nothing worth mentioning."

The two soldiers walked silently to the far side of the camp. They reached a cement building with no windows. The officer took his ID badge and ran it across a scanner. A green light came on, and the door to the building opened. The access opened to a narrow stairway that only went down. They descended. Michael read Level One on the wall, and the two men continued down the staircase to a wall marked Level Two. Again, the officer took his ID badge and swiped it across a scanner. They proceeded through a hallway with rooms on each side. The officer stopped in front of the doorway simply marked B. O. He knocked twice, and it was opened by an MP with one hand on his holstered pistol. The MP led them to an office and knocked twice.

"Come in," came the voice from inside.

Once inside, Michael found himself looking down at a weathered four-star general and then at his name plate, which read General Andrew Goodpastor.

The Captain saluted in unison with Michael and said, "Sir Private Angelino, as you ordered, sir."

The General looked into Michael's eyes with a discerning stare and, without taking his eyes off the soldier, dismissed the Captain. Once Michael's escort was gone, the General's demeanor changed.

"Sit down, Mike." The old soldier said calmly.

Michael moved into the chair by the desk, still in a state of attention.

"Relax, son." The General said softly.

11

Michael's shoulders dropped, and he tried to do as he was ordered. He was wondering what this might be about, but decided not to ask questions unless it was offered by the seasoned officer. There was silence as the four-star General looked at a screen in front of him.

Finally, the officer spoke. "I've been watching an interesting video feed of your visit to the latrine a while ago."

Michael did not react to the comment.

The General continued. "You handle yourself very well, but I have a few questions for you, son. Why did you turn your back on your attackers?"

Michael answered without much emotion. "The threat had been eliminated."

The General rubbed his right eyebrow with his index finger and asked, "How did you know for sure?"

Michael leaned closer to the desk and said almost in a whisper, "The first assailant was met with a severe blow to the neck, which I knew would cause laryngeal spasm. His biggest concern after that was breathing. The second man I knew would react to the heel of my foot making contact with his extensor hallucis brevis muscle, which gave me just enough time to strike his nose hard enough to cause unconsciousness. The final blow to the already gasping soldier was to attack the strike zone in his groin. I was convinced it would be enough to make certain the soldier was placed into a deep sleep. After that, I reasoned it might be a good idea to finish what I started, Sir."

The General leaned back in his chair with his hands behind his neck. "Very impressive..." He said as he continued to carefully study the face of the Private. There was a small silence. The General sat upright at his desk and made a proposal to Michael.

"How would you like to join a unique group of soldiers for very special assignments?" Michael thought this might be the perfect opportunity to declare his desire to be a medic and get a positive response.

"Well, Sir, I enlisted in the service to become a medic and help save lives. Does this assignment have anything to do with that?"

The General looked at the young man, thought for a moment, and said, "Well, son...not exactly, but in this type of work, the end result would be that you will probably save hundreds, maybe even thousands of lives."

Michael had a vague suspicion of where this was leading, and finally asked to hear more about it. The General smiled at the young soldier.

"Michael, you possess the kind of skills that we need to make a stronger impact on the war. There are just a few men who have passed the very select requirements we need for this assignment I'm offering you. May I be blunt, son?" His tone became much more serious. "Our enemy leaders are hell bent to not only kill as many of our men as they can but to humiliate and denigrate our soldiers to the point of despair. They do not engage in a war according to the Geneva Convention. They spit on the rules of war. There are no front lines in Viet Nam, and the enemy has an intricate tunnel system that allows them to pop up almost anywhere. In short, we are getting our asses kicked. It has been determined that a new approach needs to be employed, but it is one that cannot be recognized by our code of conduct. You would be trained to live alone and apart from the regular troops. You would be invisible and a part of the jungle in which you will reside. There will be contact points where you will receive Intel regarding a particular mission. Sometimes you will work alone, other times you may have forces with you, or sometimes just a shadow. There will be no rules to follow or any guidelines on how to accomplish your missions; we are only interested in the results. You will be a government assassin, but if caught, we will put out information that you were AWOL from your designated unit and that your actions were those of a mentally ill soldier who could not handle the stresses of battle. You would not be afforded any assistance from the government you work for, but make no mistake about it, Michael, if you agree to this assignment, you will, in fact, be saving lives."

"Then I guess I shouldn't get caught, right, sir?" Michael asked, smiling. The General smiled back.

"Is that a yes?" The General queried.

Michael wanted to say yes to the General, but something in his soul told him he needed to counsel with his parish priest, Father Robert Pinta. Michael was strong in his faith and was being asked to become a government murderer. He had been an altar boy and Father Pinta, and they had become very close friends over the years. Whenever Michael had concerns, the priest either gave him scripture to read or questions to ponder so that he would find the answers he needed.

"I need to discuss this with my confessor before I make a commitment, sir. You're asking me to go against commandments I believe were given to me by God."

The General smiled again at the young soldier. "Michael, take the weekend to speak to your priest. I'm asking you to risk your life for your country, and you need to be sure of your decision, because son, any indecision will get you killed." The General remarked sincerely.

Both men stood, and the General put out his hand. They shook hands, and then Michael saluted the General and left the office.

Michael slowly walked back to his barracks. He wasn't sure he could do what was asked by the General. He thought to himself. "How would God feel about me killing people for the government?" As he entered the barracks, there sitting quietly in his office was Sergeant Harris, two fingers tapping diligently on his typewriter. Without raising his head, he asked, "What do you think, Mike?" Michael was surprised at the informal question.

He answered, "Sounds like something I would be good at, Sarge, but I'm just not sure about all it involves."

Sergeant Harris waved the young recruit to come inside his office and close the door. He spent the next two hours detailing what the job involved, focusing on what the results meant to the troops who might never know he was there. Later that night, the young soldier positioned himself on his bunk and read from his Bible.

Getting a pass during basic training was hardly ever allowed, but Michael found himself on a Greyhound bus heading for his hometown. When he arrived at the station, he walked over to Elizabeth's house. She screamed, running out the screen door as she saw him coming toward the house in his dress uniform. She leaped, and her beautiful, long legs wrapped around his waist as she flew into his strong arms. He kissed her softly at first, then long and hard, and she kissed him right back. She told him she loved the smell of his Jade East cologne as she nuzzled her nose against his neck.

She was out of breath as she questioned him. "When did you get leave? Why didn't you call? How long will you be home? I missed you. I love you." Then she kissed him again, not giving him a chance to answer. Her arms were wrapped around his neck, her fingers rubbed his very short haircut, and at the same time, she kissed him, and the combination made him tingle down to his toes.

Between kisses, he was able to get out, "I love you."

They sat and talked for a while. He knew there was nothing he could tell her regarding the decision he had to make. They talked instead about how they felt about each other and things regarding the life they were planning for their future together. After an hour, Michael told her he needed to get home to see his Mom and Pop.

"Elle, can I borrow your car for an hour?"

She got the keys from her purse and handed them to him. "Come pick me up when you're done," Elle said, kissing him.

He was telling her the truth, but his next stop was St. Bridget's Catholic Church. Father Bob was expecting him. He walked into the house of worship; his footsteps echoing as he made his way to the confessional. There were just a few old people in line to confess their transgressions. Michael thought to himself, "They look too old to sin." He moved into a pew and closed his eyes to get his thoughts together. He opened them when he felt a tap on his shoulder. There in front of him was Father Robert Pinta. He was a tall, thin man, just over six feet. He had a crooked smile, light brown eyes, and a clean-shaven face. His hair was almost as short as Michael's, but he used some butch wax to make an impressive crew cut.

"Were you planning to confess today?" The priest said, smiling.

"Sorry Father...I was just thinking about things." Michael said quietly.

"Let's go to my office, Mike. I really don't think this is a confessional kind of talk." Father Bob said softly as he placed his hand on the young soldier's shoulder.

Michael had spent the better part of an hour describing in detail what would be expected of him when he took the military assignment. He was questioning the result this would have on his immortal soul. The priest lit a cigarette, listening patiently as his long-time altar boy expressed concern over what he should do to make peace with his decision.

"I guess what I need is some reassurance that I'm not condemning myself to an eternity in hell," Michael concluded.

The priest took a moment to gather his thoughts; then, finally, he began to speak.

"Mike, this is a time of war. Every day, the reports come in that hundreds of American soldiers are dying on the battlefield. From what you have told me, it appears your officers believe that your efforts might help bring those numbers down. The danger to yourself will be great, and you could die. The big question is...are you willing to sacrifice yourself in an effort to save others? Our Lord said, "*Greater love has no one than this that he lay down his life for his friends*." There is one more thing to evaluate, Mike. Your superiors have determined that out of all the soldiers in that camp, they believe you can do this job. They aren't looking for a martyr. They think they have found someone who can win. I think they're right. "Mike, I've known you most of your life. I know you believe with all your heart that Jesus Christ is your savior and that through his death on the cross, He paid your sin debt. The question is, what if you know that killing is a sin and you continue to commit that sin? Christ's death paid for your sins, past, present, and future. I believe your soul is secure. Your job is to bring other souls to God, but where you're going, you probably won't have much time for that. So make it your goal to come home and work for God." Michael nodded with a deeper understanding as the priest continued.

"Go home and pray on it tonight. The peace you're seeking will come to you."

The priest embraced him, then walked the soldier to his car. Michael turned to his priest, shook his hand firmly, and said, "Thanks, Father." Again, the priest embraced the young man, he watched him grow up and said, "You will be prayed for in every mass I say until you come home." Michael got into his car and drove away. Father Bob lit another cigarette as he watched the car disappear around the corner.

Michael took a walk with his father. "Che cosa è errato il mio figlio? What's bothering you so badly?" His father asked. Michael answered his father with the details of his assignment. "I wanted you to know, in case something happens and you hear that I was crazy, you will know the truth. Mom will be out of her mind, and you can at least reassure her that I was doing my job."

"Siete sicuro questo siete che cosa volete fare? Are you sure?" His father asked as his hand touched his son's face gently. "Yes, Pop, I'm sure it's what I want to do," Michael assured his father. Then his father kissed him. "Ti Amo. I love you." Michael answered him, "Anche e ti amo."

The weekend pass was over much too quickly for Michael, but he was glad to have spent some quality time with his parents. His mother made all his favorite dishes, but cried every time she thought of him leaving. Elizabeth was harder to say goodbye to because his heart ached when he was away from her. When she asked what he would be trained to do, he was ambiguous because he didn't want her to worry. He had made peace with his decision. He decided he would tell her everything after it was all over, sure that the details would only make it worse for her.

Chapter One: Rough Day

Sitting at his standard-issue cherry wood desk in a rather small office on the third floor, level C, of the Pentagon, Michael Angelino, FBI agent, chewed on a pencil as he pondered the distressing news that had arrived earlier. A top secret document read: ***Attack Eminent!*** The source gave no particulars, but intimated a Middle Eastern involvement. Michael had already sent word to all his field agents to gather as much intelligence as possible so he could put a tangible scenario together for the military brass. His team had already been made aware that something was brewing, something really big, but nothing concrete had been found. Communication with the CIA was futile, and his superiors would be expecting intelligent information by tomorrow. Michael didn't like not knowing what was going on and needed the most up-to-date fact gathering he could get his hands on. He already had an idea that it was Al-Qaeda. His first priority was to recognize where the attack would take place and how they might prevent it from happening. The preliminary reports were sporadic, and other than the Middle Eastern connection, nothing specific had been found, but the internet chatter from that area was almost constant. Michael wanted to know where the U.S. Navy had ships within the Saudi region. They had attacked the Navy before, so that seemed the most intelligent avenue to travel.

Michael stared at the framed black and white picture of his hero, General William T. Sherman, when Tess Lamia, his second in command and someone he trusted with his life, walked in. She was a vision of loveliness, with shiny black hair that draped just over her shoulders and beautiful, almond-shaped blue eyes that always sparkled when she spoke to him. Her curves were obvious in her gray pencil skirt and white sheer blouse, and her legs were long and very shapely in passion red heels. Michael didn't notice her at first, still lost in thought.

"Hey Mike, where were you just now?" She questioned as he continued to stare at the picture.

He was brought to the here and now by her question. He looked over at her, thought a minute, and then answered.

"I was just wondering what the General would think of the way we're handling ourselves in today's world." Their eyes met. They both smiled briefly at each other. Michael's eyes moved back to the picture, as he knew he could easily get lost in hers.

"Pretty different world from the one he was dealing with, isn't it?" She asked.

Michael thought for a moment. "Not really, Tess." Michael continued. "Two ideologies with people on both sides willing to die to defend them. Not so different. Of course, today the enemy can kill thousands in just a few minutes, and we have allowed politicians to get themselves into the middle of something they not only don't comprehend, but something none of them have the stomach for, because no matter how you decorate what's going on right now, it is a war. The bombing of the USS Cole in 2000 and the killing of seventeen U.S. soldiers made it a war. Now, you can bet your life that this Al-Qaeda group is planning something else, and it will be another suicide mission, because to these misguided zealots it is an obligation to God." He responded with a patriotic tone.

She nodded with understanding; then changed the subject. "Are you ready to leave your wife for me?"

He answered without missing a beat. "Can't today, it's our thirty-second anniversary, but thanks so much for asking." They smiled at each other again.

Tess restarted the conversation. "Avery wants to have a meeting about the latest intelligence we received in about twenty minutes, okay?" He nodded as he watched her face. She turned and gave him a seductive look as she was leaving his office. He watched her sashay down the hall after his glass door closed. She was a beauty, but taking it any further than their casual sexual innuendo would screw up his very happy marriage.

Michael knew there was something between them, but the love of his life was Elizabeth Angelino, and tonight he would be making her a wonderful lasagna dinner.

He put the mauled pencil down and leaned back into his office chair. "Thirty-two years, where did all that time go? Wasn't it just yesterday when I was a young man?"

Michael's mind had been reliving his past all day. Absentmindedly, he reached into the oven to check on his lasagna and burned his finger lifting the sheet of aluminum covering his Mama's secret recipe. He retreated, quickly swinging his hand through the air, on his way to the sink and the relief of cold tap water on his burn. He was working on a limited time schedule and wanted everything to be just right for their anniversary. He thought to himself, "Thirty-two years, gone in an instant." He dried his hands and put on an oven mitt, rechecked the main course, and closed the door of the appliance. Michael looked back at his finger and decided he had better get a Band-Aid from the bathroom. He went through the dining room and gave it a once-over; lace tablecloth, bouquet of thirty-two red roses, one for each year, in a beautiful crystal vase, the table set for two, even their best crystal and silverware. The room was just the way he wanted it. He just needed to light the candles. He looked at his finger, angry that it was still throbbing with pain, and made his way to the bathroom. Michael had just closed the medicine cabinet after taping his digit when the phone rang.

"Hello, Michael Angelino here." He announced into the receiver.

"Sorry, sweetheart, I've got a few more charts to finish, and I'll be home." Elizabeth apologized.

"It's okay, but I burned my finger and will need a nurse as soon as possible." He said jokingly.

"Cold water and a band-aid should hold you." She prescribed it to her husband.

"Elle, have I told you that I love you today?" He asked.

"I think four times, so far, but who's counting!" She giggled into the phone and then continued, "Let me go, so I can get out of here."

"See you in a few," he answered her and hung up the phone.

Elizabeth Angelino had been an ER nurse for almost twenty-five years at Gettysburg Hospital. She never had to stay late to finish charts, but it had always been a great excuse if she needed to do things after work. On this day, Elle, as Michael still affectionately called her, needed to check in with her doctor. She left her unit, rubbing her hands with dreaded anticipation. She went to the elevator and pressed two. As the doors closed, she nervously shook her hands as if they were wet. When the elevator opened, she walked quickly down the hallway. She stopped in front of a frosted glass entrance. It read OB GYN Department. She looked in each direction to ensure she wasn't being seen by anyone, and then quickly walked inside. The doctor was speaking to the receptionist when Elizabeth approached the desk. Dr. Emory McKinney looked up and said, "Hi Liz, let's go into my office."

Once they were both seated, the doctor pulled out a chart and began to review the test results. "Liz, I am still waiting for the CA-125 blood tests, but I believe we're looking at ovarian cancer. When those results come in, we will determine how aggressive we will need to be and what procedures we will have to do. Have you spoken to your husband?"

Liz looked down and shook her head. "No, Michael has been so busy with the Bureau, I hate worrying him until I know for sure."

"You need to talk with him soon, Liz. You've put this off too long already," The doctor instructed her sternly.

"I know, but today is our anniversary. I'll tell him tomorrow, one day won't matter." Liz said, smiling at the doctor.

"Okay, I'll call you tomorrow. I should have the test results by then. Are you working?" Dr. McKinney inquired.

"Seven to seven thirty," Liz responded with a nod.

They both got up from their chairs and moved toward the door of the doctor's office. McKinney shook her hand and then placed his other hand over hers. "Alright, I'll call you in the ER tomorrow, Liz. Happy Anniversary." He smiled affectionately at her as she departed. When she had gone, Emory sat back down and looked again at the file, shaking his head with sadness on his face. Gina, his receptionist, entered his office to pick up the file.

"Nurses are so busy caring for others that they forget themselves." Dr. Emory said solemnly as he handed Gina the chart.

Michael saw the headlights as Elle's car pulled up. He grabbed a lighter, lit the candles, and then made his way to the door. He smiled to himself when he realized that he still got excited at the thought of seeing her. She was his world, his soul mate, and his best friend. "Happy Anniversary, Elle." He sang as she came through the door. He wrapped his arms around her, kissed her softly, and then with passion.

"You are the best kisser." She said, catching her breath. Elizabeth looked over his shoulder and saw the candlelit table filled with red roses. She began to cry because she loved him so much and because she didn't know if she would ever have another anniversary. Michael saw her emotion. "Hope you're hungry." She turned back to him and kissed him hard, holding his face with her hands. "My God, I love you." She said as she continued to hold his face.

Escorted to her dining room chair, Elizabeth looked up, surprised as Michael pulled it out for her. "What is that marvelous smell coming from the kitchen?" Elizabeth questioned. Michael ran for the oven, concerned. Yelling back at her, "It's my special garlic cheese bread." A few moments later, Michael appeared with two plates of lasagna in one hand and a bowl of sliced garlic cheese bread in the other. Elle gave him an impressed look. He responded, "Maybe I should have been a waiter." He carefully placed the dishes on the table, leaned over, and kissed her, "Happy Anniversary, sweetheart."

After dinner, he moved their wine glasses to the coffee table in the living room. Elle followed him into the room, unsure of what he had planned but willing to comply with anything he asked her to do. Michael went to the stereo and put on a record. As the music started,

Michael turned and began to sing along with Neil Diamond. "Stay for just a while...stay and let me look at you...it's been so long I hardly knew you standing in the door." He let Neil take over and put his hand out to her.

"Wanna dance?" Elle took his hand as he led her to the floor. He embraced her as they moved around the room. Looked into her beautiful eyes and said, "I'm pretty sure Neil must have written this song for us. I wanted you so bad when I got back from Nam. I wanted to tear your clothes off and make love to you until we couldn't walk. I had thought about you every day as I went through that hell. You were my redemption. I had become uncivilized in those 18 months, taking what I needed when I needed it. Then I was home, unpacking my clothes, and there you were standing in my doorway, more beautiful than I ever even imagined you could be. I didn't want to frighten you, and that other part of me would have sent you away screaming. It's a part of me I never want to see again."

Elle put her finger over his lips, then moved her hand around his neck and kissed him passionately. It was all he needed to put that part of his past behind him and embrace his now. They found their way to the bedroom and made love to each other with years of experience and total understanding of each other's needs and wants.

The all too familiar sound of the bedside alarm made its morning announcement clearly as Michael Angelino pressed the off button. His body slowly made its way to the kitchen. Arms mechanically moved to the cupboard and removed the coffee and its corresponding filter. The faucet at the sink responded to the hand's contact. The pot received a quick rinsing before being filled over the ten-cup mark. The coffee machine accepted its required liquid minus the customary spillage, and the red light meant he would be awake soon. He stole a cup by replacing his cup with the glass pot. It was a trick his wife Elizabeth taught him years ago. He rubbed his slightly protruding belly as the coffee found his lips. Then he suddenly found himself standing by the kitchen window staring out. This is where consciousness replaced his unconscious morning ritual.

The aroma of freshly brewed coffee suddenly reached her nose. Elizabeth's eyes opened as a result. Elle heard the shower going. She smiled as she stretched her sore arms and legs from yesterday's twelve-hour shift at the hospital and a wonderful night of lovemaking. Today would make her fifth twelve-hour shift in as many days, but after today, she would have six days off, and that meant some quality time with the man she loved. She headed for the kitchen.

Michael stepped out of the shower as Elle staggered in with a coffee cup in hand. She placed her cup on the bathroom counter and began to step out of her pajamas. Michael shook his wet head. The cold water had its effect on Elle's naked body, and she instinctively slapped his shoulder as she made her way into the shower.

"You can't keep this up, you know," Michael said loudly over the sound of running water.

"I know!" She responded.

"You were wonderful last night…made me feel like a young buck again," Michael said as he ran a brush through what little hair he had on his head, followed by brushing through his beard. Elle came out of the shower and hugged him with her wet body. He turned quickly and kissed her lips, then her neck. He moved farther down to her wet breast and sucked gently. "Easy, big boy, they're a bit sore this morning." She giggled as she pulled away.

"Oh, by the way..." She remembered. "We have a committee meeting tonight at the parish about the charity bazaar. Please don't be too late."

"I won't. I'm in meetings all day today at the Pentagon; things are getting hectic there." Michael said. He tried to grab her bottom as she ran through the bathroom door, but was unsuccessful. He yelled after her, "That means I'll have plenty of energy for a repeat performance of last night." Elizabeth smiled and said under her breath, "If you don't fall asleep on the couch."

Michael put on a dark blue suit, a starched white shirt, a blue and black striped silk tie, a black belt, socks, and shoes. He went into the kitchen and stood there waiting for a response. Elle was buttering English muffins when she smelled his Obsession cologne. She looked up and rolled her eyes, saying, "Wow!" Michael questioned almost seriously. "Have you ever noticed that as men get older, they begin to look better in clothes rather than out of clothes?" Elizabeth smiled, lifting her eyebrows, "Too much lasagna." She put a muffin in his mouth; then tapped on his stomach lightly. "We need to start dieting again, so enjoy this muffin, it will be your last for a while."

Michael quickly changed the subject. "I want to ask Father O'Reilly about starting a Bible study. Elizabeth commented with a giggle. "Better be careful. You'll turn all the Catholics into Protestants if they start reading the Bible."

"Very funny." He pretended to laugh. "If people read their Bible more, maybe there would be less violence to deal with in the world. I'm not kidding, Elle, the church isn't putting any emphasis on how much the Bible speaks to us in our daily life. How will the next generation of Christians get by if they aren't in tune with what the Bible says is coming into the world?" Elle hadn't commented, Michael noticed.

Elle sipped her coffee and stared out the window. She had become preoccupied with something. Michael gave her some space. A few minutes went by. She continued looking out into the yard; then said quietly, "Josh called yesterday." Michael looked down briefly; his demeanor changed. He stiffened with tension and then inquired, "How is he?"

Elizabeth responded with a bit of anger. "Why are you two so stubborn? Do you even know what you're fighting about?" Michael answered her. "We're not fighting. He just doesn't think I'm someone he wants to be like or spend time with. That's okay, I get it. He's busy with his west-coast friends, and I'm just an old, how did he say it? Oh yeah, he said I was a pencil pusher who wastes all his free time in church." Elizabeth held his arm affectionately and said, "He's just a kid." Michael put his hand over hers, looked into her eyes, and said, "No, Elle, he isn't a kid anymore, but it hurts me because he doesn't respect the person I am."

"Call him Mike," Elizabeth begged.

"He's got my number, Elle," Michael responded coldly.

Michael kissed his wife. "I'll see you at the church tonight."

Elizabeth Angelino waved goodbye to her husband, glad that he could not see her tears. The thought of her beloved being alone was more than she could handle. If the test results were bad, he would need Josh just as much as Josh would need him. If she had waited too long to get medical attention, they would have needed each other badly. She picked up the phone to call her son, but realizing that it was three hours earlier, she replaced the receiver. She thought to herself, "This is going to be a rough day."

Michael was listening to talk radio as he was driving when the report came in that an airliner had just struck one of the twin towers in New York. Instinctively, his foot stepped on the gas. He put in a call to Tess, who answered on the first ring.

"Michael, where are you?" came the voice from the phone.

"I'm about ten minutes out. What reports are we getting?" Michael barked back.

"The reports are sketchy, but our sources indicate an American Airlines flight 11 from Boston en route to L.A. struck the north tower of the World Trade Center in downtown New York, just before nine. The airline is trying to determine if there were problems with the instruments on board." Tess informed her boss.

"It's an attack, Tess. Get word to move the President now." Michael screamed into the phone and then hung up as he raced his car into the Pentagon parking structure. His VIP status there gave him a parking place close to the river entrance.

He made his way through the descending alphabetized hallway, which was extra busy with personnel moving from one corridor to another. He rushed through the A section door into the courtyard as military and civilian employees rushed in every direction, reentering section A of the Westside wing. He made his way up three flights of stairs to the third floor. He knowingly moved through the labyrinth of corridors until he was looking at Tess waiting by his office door. Their regular banter with sexual innuendo was lost as the grave situation had just gotten worse. Tess handed him some papers as they both made their way into the conference room, already filled with Pentagon personnel. Michael immediately took charge of the meeting with a question. "Has the President been moved?" A three-star general answered. "He is being taken to Air Force One as we speak." Michael began the meeting by discussing the possibility of more attacks. The room was tense, as reports came in from intelligence that something more was brewing. All of a sudden, the teleprompter was showing film footage of the plane making contact with the tower. Gasps filled the room as the newscaster on the scene began to report that this was, in fact, the south tower, which had just been hit.

"Let's go, people," Michael screamed across the room. Contact the FAC, all aircraft need to be on the ground as soon as possible, and get the F-14s in the air around the city. The conference room cleared as military and civilian workers went to work trying to determine who was attacking us and why.

Michael leaned closer to Tess and whispered, "It's not over yet." Tess looked at him with fear in her eyes, "Are you kidding me?"

Michael started to answer when his cell phone began to ring.

"It's Elle," Michael said as he raised his hand, motioning Tess to hold on. She gave him a signal that she would get back to him and headed down the hallway. Michael couldn't help but watch her as she moved away from him. She was such a beautiful woman, and under different circumstances, he was sure he could get himself in trouble.

"Hey, Elle, are you watching the insanity?" He said calmly. Elle knew the more calm Michael was, the worse the situation.

She asked him, "Mike, what is going on?"

His response was somber and brought on a fear she couldn't comprehend. "It's the beginning of something big and probably very bad. Can't really talk right now, but I'll call you as things develop. I love you."

She told him she loved him, too, just as paramedics brought in a patient complaining of severe chest pain into her emergency room. Paramedic Tom Shaw reported that the 62-year-old male had been watching the news when he suddenly felt like an elephant was sitting on his chest. Elizabeth got the patient immediately hooked up to the heart monitor when she heard another ambulance approaching the ER. "How many more will be rolling in because of the horror in New York?" She thought to herself.

Michael was walking back down the C corridor in the direction of the south entrance when the floor beneath his feet shook violently, knocking him to the floor, and the sound of a massive explosion filled his ears just as his head struck the floor. Michael didn't know how long he had been knocked out. As he came to, he looked back toward where he had been and saw nothing but black smoke filling the hallway. In that instant, something strange happened to him; he felt as if he were back in Viet Nam. He could hear screaming coming from where the smoke was and went into a kind of autopilot mode. His new mission was to extract his comrades. He quickly covered his face with a handkerchief he pulled from his pocket and moved low to the ground toward the sound of pain. He found his way to a small office where a dark cherry wood bookcase had been knocked over. He crawled to where a young officer was lying and felt for a pulse. When none was found, he continued to move across the floor of the room. He saw a pair of legs moving from under a desk and approached, asking, "Can you move?" The answer was weak. "My arm is stuck." A female voice said as she coughed from the smoke. Michael found the point of contact and lifted the desk with his back, pulling the arm free with his hands. "Let's get the fuck out of here." He said as he dragged her across the room below the smoke. Once outside the office, he scooped her up and headed down the stairs, the woman in his arms. He dropped her off at the courtyard and returned to his floor. Again, he got close to the ground and moved toward the smoke-filled hallway. One by one, Michael brought survivors out onto the steps of the courtyard. In his mind, he was not at the Pentagon but back in Viet Nam. He was trying to save lives. A television van was already on the scene with cameras capturing the horrible destruction of an airline passenger plane making contact with the brain center of the American military. After about thirty minutes into the operation, he was confronted as he dropped off another victim of the explosion. A fireman told him he must evacuate the building immediately. Michael, in his confused state, only saw this person as an enemy combatant. He responded to the directive by ripping the helmet off the hose man and swinging around quickly, his right elbow striking the face of the surprised firefighter, who instantly fell unconscious at Michael's feet. Michael took the helmet and jacket from the fireman and reentered the building. He was calling out into the smoke, "If you can hear me call out." Room by room, he crawled across the floors. He heard the voice of a woman. She was moaning. He found her under a desk, her leg bleeding from what looked like a compound fracture as the bone tore through the surface of her skin. The room was a shambles with furniture shattered by the force of the disaster. He quickly ripped the hem of her skirt, rolled up part of it, handed it to her, and said firmly, "Bite down on this." She fearfully did as he instructed. His hands moved rapidly, pulling her leg to a straightened position, bringing the bone back into a proper alignment. The woman fainted from the painful maneuver. He then took part of the torn hem and wrapped it around the wound. He found an electrical cord and two small pieces of wood from the debris and made a splint. He put the woman over his shoulder and headed down the stairs. Halfway down, she became conscious and began moaning with pain. He began to console her just as they came to an approaching ambulance.

He dropped her off at the open back end, a paramedic jumping out to help him. As he leaned over to place her gently on the gurney, his helmet fell off. When she got a look at him, she yelled, "Mike!" Suddenly, Michael Angelino was back at the Pentagon. He was unaware of anything since he said goodbye to Elizabeth. He saw Tess lying on the stretcher and asked her what had happened. She immediately turned to the medic and said, "He's coming with us."

With no memory of what had happened, the hospital began running tests to determine if the head injury he incurred caused a concussion. Tess was taken to the orthopedic section of the emergency room, where the doctor was quite impressed with the reduction of the compound fracture and the crude splint on her leg. The X-ray showed that the bone was in perfect alignment. The technician had only to clean and dress her wound and put her in a removable cast. The two comrades finally met in the hallway of the emergency room.

"How are you feeling, Mike?" Tess questioned with real concern.

"I'm okay, just a headache. I can't remember anything after the explosion." He explained to her. She told him that earlier, he didn't remember the explosion.

"Your memory might come back when that bump on your head goes down. You could have a concussion." She told her boss.

"What hit the building? Was it another aircraft?" He asked, almost sure of the answer.

"I heard it was an American Airlines flight with about sixty-five passengers. Then there was another flight they think was headed for the Capitol or the White House, but it went down somewhere southeast of Pittsburgh around ten o'clock, and they don't seem to know why." Tess reported to her boss.

Michael thought about Elle and what she must be thinking. He reached into his pocket and pulled out his cell phone in pieces and remarked. "Well, this isn't going to work."

The Gettysburg Hospital emergency room was filled beyond capacity with patients occupying extra gurneys in the hallway. Elizabeth was delegating nurses to triage patients when the report that the Pentagon had been struck by another airliner. She tried to reach Michael repeatedly but was getting no response. Elizabeth was taking the blood pressure of a new patient when her cell phone buzzed. She finished taking vitals on the patient, pulled the curtain, and looked quickly to see who called her, hoping it was Michael. It was her son, Joshua. She redialed his number. He answered immediately. "Mom," The voice of her son called out nervously. "Did you see him?"

"Your Dad?" She questioned.

"Yes, I was sitting in my office when I saw him on the television. The news has video of him bringing people out of the Pentagon. Mom, he dropped one off and ran back inside. He must have brought out eight to ten people. I didn't think Dad could lift anything but a Bible." The voice on the phone began to crackle with emotion. "I'm such a jerk. I could have lost him today and not told him how much I love him. I'm so sorry, Mom. Please tell him I'm sorry. I'm so sorry." Her son couldn't speak anymore as he was reduced to sobbing into the phone.

Elizabeth spoke softly into the receiver. "Josh, it's alright, if you saw Dad, then he's okay, and that's the most important thing. I have to go, but I'll call you later as soon as he calls me. I love you."

She hung up the phone, relieved that at least Michael was alive. She worked less stressed, but was concerned that he hadn't gotten word to her. The thought that something else might happen was beginning to fester when her cell phone rang. She looked down and saw the call was from Tess Lamia. When she put the phone to her ear, she heard the voice of the man she loved.

"Elle?" His voice questioned.

"Mike, are you okay? Josh said he saw you on a news report." She voiced concern.

Mike answered her calmly. "I'm fine Elle. I just don't remember much of what happened. I have a big bump on the side of my head. I remember talking with you and was heading back to the conference room when the explosion occurred. That's where the memory gets hazy."

"Have you gotten checked for a head injury?" The nurse part of her questioned.

"Yes, but so far they have found nothing to be concerned about, but I will be here for a while. I think they are going to do an MRI. Tess is with me. She broke her leg, and she has the only surviving phone between us." He said, trying to make her laugh.

Elizabeth was concerned about his loss of memory, but she could tell he still had his sense of humor. "Alright then, do I need to come and get you at some point?"

He responded quickly. "I'll call you if that should be the case; otherwise, I'll be home sometime tonight. Love you Elle."

"Love you back." She said, hanging up. Then Elizabeth sat down in the emergency room and cried with relief.

Michael did not make it home that night. Upon release from the hospital, he found himself in a bunker just outside of Washington, D.C. He and Tess, on crutches, were attempting to put together all the pieces of the most horrible attack on U.S. soil since World War II. Information began to filter in that this was the work of Al-Qaeda and was masterminded by Osama bin Laden. This Islamic extremist in 1998 had declared a jihad against all infidels, regardless of whether they were military or civilian, and issued a religious order that it was the holy duty of all Muslims to kill Americans wherever possible. The CIA had provided information that the FBI should have had prior to the attack, but Michael didn't want the meeting to turn into a *"who's to blame"* exchange. It was more important to begin to make some sense out of the chaos and to prevent further possible attacks.

By the time the meeting ended, the sun was already making its way across the sky, and his wife would be distraught. He used a landline within the bunker. "Elle, I'm coming home." He spoke softly into the phone, expecting her to scream her concerns.

She answered, "You'll probably be hungry. I'll start cooking. It should be ready when you get here. Are you okay?"

"Just tired." He said.

"Okay, I'll see you soon…love you," she said; then hung up the phone. This was the worst day of her life. She couldn't stop crying when she thought of all the innocent people who had died and all the loved ones who still didn't know one way or the other. She prayed a prayer of thanks to God for sparing her husband as she moved with purpose around the kitchen. She tried to keep herself busy until she heard the front door open. She ran into his arms and kissed him over and over again all over his face. Her tears wet his face as her lips moved all over. Once she found his lips, she kissed him hard. He knew that he had almost been taken from her, and so he kissed her back just as hard. She was right. It had been a rough day.

Chapter Two: Revenge

The badly tortured man pleaded for his life, but he had disobeyed a direct order from a man whose desire for revenge was far beyond the required jihad directed by Osama Bin Laden. Zafeer El-Amin continued to strike his disobedient soldier over and over again with each fist, causing horrible damage. Once unconscious, his attacker continued to pound the soldier's face, a word for each blow, while the other men in the room looked on solemnly. "I" A bash to his jaw made a cracking noise. "Will," A punch to the nose produced squirting blood. "Not." A backhand with his ring finger tore the flesh from the left side of his face. "Tolerate." Another fist jerked the soldier's head in the opposite direction. "Incompetence." The final whack was a strike to the top of the man's head, which broke his neck and brought him to death. Zafeer kicked the man, causing his chair to fall backwards onto the hardwood floor.

"Clean up this mess!" He yelled into the room. The soldiers reacted instantly, all fearful that they could be next, so two men picked up the limp body. The other two men used towels to clean the bloodied floor.

"Khalil, how could that idiot miss the plane? The Golden Gate Bridge should have been in the San Francisco Bay today. These American infidels should have seen that they were in danger from coast to coast." Zafeer shouted to his second in command.

Khalil Nadiman, his second in command, tried to explain, "Zafeer, he was held up at the rental return, and then the shuttle broke down."

"I'm tired of depending on others. I will exact revenge in my own way from now on." Zafeer spoke loudly into the room.

The eight Middle Eastern men in the room echoed support for their leader, which he relished; then he told Khalil to clear the area so he could think.

Once the room had cleared, Zafeer sat on the leather couch, pulled out a picture of his mother, and told Khalil he would soon deliver a new plan against the American pigs.

"Leave me, Khalil," Zafeer said quietly as he gazed upon the picture.

Khalil had seen him begin to get emotional only one other time, and he knew to give him some space.

Zafeer's tears obstructed his view of his beautiful mother. He wiped his eyes as he remembered the last time he saw her.

Jessina El-Amin was, as her name implied, a flower. She was twenty-seven when she arrived with her husband, Abdul, and son, Zafeer, to Libya to visit her cousin at the palatial military compound of Colonel Muammar Gaddafi known as Bab al-Aziziya. They would be staying at a diplomatic compound in Tripoli.

The United States and Gaddafi relations brought U. S. Secretary of State and European and Arab partners to agree that force must be shown against the leader who was taking credit for terrorist attacks in Vienna, Rome, and Berlin. President Reagan called for an air strike against the military compound with the intention of showing that force would be used against Gaddafi. The Colonel was warned that a strike would take place to minimize casualties, so he had all visitors removed from the complex.

Abdul and his family were told to stay inside their quarters until the raid was over. Hearing a loud noise just after two in the morning, Zafeer got up and made his way to his mother and father's room, when the ceiling of the building began to fall in upon him. Frightened, he leaned against one of the white alabaster pillars that lined the hallway, as debris and dust filled the room. He ran as fast as he could to find his parents. His eyes fought to see through the dust of rubble falling all around him. She was in her bed, motionless.

"Mother, Mother!" He called out.

Zafeer ran to her bedside and saw she was severely bleeding from a wound on her head. He immediately saw a large piece of the ceiling by her side of the bed. He grabbed her hand, which was limp but still warm in his. Zafeer began to scream over and over, calling out for her to wake up. A soldier saw the young boy and scooped him up in his arms, and ran for cover as the room continued to be assaulted by bombs. Zafeer called out to her lifeless body as he was carried away. He wanted to hear her voice one last time, but there was no sound. He was in the Gaddafi bunker with many others when word came that the attack was by the American Navy and Air Force. He had decided at that moment that he would avenge his mother's death against those who killed her, and it would be something America would never forget.

He put the picture back into his wallet, reached into his pants, and took out a handkerchief. He wiped his eyes and wiped the dead man's blood from his hands. Zafeer El-Amin had finally been in a position to exact revenge for the death of his mother, and he could not let incompetence be tolerated in this quest for vengeance. He had studied too hard and practiced the art of terrorism for too many years in the deserts of Pakistan. Bin Laden had called him a true zealot for the cause of Islam. In truth, Zafeer couldn't care less about the goals of Al Qaeda. His only reason for aligning himself with these fanatics was to put himself in the right place to accomplish his personal mission, and that was to destroy American families just as his family had been destroyed.

"Khalil, we must move tonight to a location of safety as we develop a new attack plan on America," Zafeer yelled through the wall.

The door opened quickly as his second in command entered. "Will we be awaiting orders from our leader?" Khalil asked.

"All future orders will come from me, Khalil."

His subordinate nodded with complete loyalty, turned to the soldiers, and told them to pack for an immediate departure.

The terrorists had been staying in Hawaii at the beautiful and expensive Royal Kona Resort, which overlooked Kailua Bay, and under different circumstances, Zafeer would have enjoyed the relaxed atmosphere of this tropical paradise, but it was also a part of the country he hated. So, leaving it would not be that hard to do.

Khalil asked his superior where they would go. He was told to get tickets for their crew on four different flights to Mexico City. They were to avoid confrontation at any cost. They were instructed to shave their beards and get short haircuts.

"You will accompany the first group. Make arrangements at the Four Seasons Hotel. We will take a small vacation until security worldwide goes down." Zafeer instructed. "Then the moment they become complacent again, we will remind them they are infidels, only this time I want the blood of millions, not only a few thousand."

Within a few days, the group of terrorists had settled into their new temporary home, a luxurious five-star hotel right in the heart of Mexico City. They had been well-financed by Al Qaeda, so they lived like the rich and famous. Zafeer was presenting himself to the local bankers as an entrepreneur interested in establishing a manufacturing business in their industrial district or investing in one. Mr. Juan Ortiz, president of Banco di México, set up meetings with existing manufacturers to see how they might be able to help what might mean new money to their starving city of over seven million, and large deposits for his bank.

After a number of exchanges with local industrialists, Zafeer approached Mr. Ortiz about investing his money in a company that focused on steel production. Industrias CH, S.A.R. de M.V. was a company started in the early thirties, that had come on hard times and was looking for a venture capitalist to invest money to help them with a double-digit growth spurt they themselves could not support. The terrorist would establish himself as a legitimate businessman while he worked on how he would exact devastation on America. It did not take him long to find out how easily anyone in this country could be bought for the right price. So finding mercenaries was not hard and took no time at all. Zafeer needed a plan. He looked at his map of the United States and saw the city of Galveston as a location to check out, as it was a major seaport for oil and natural gas production. He thought to himself, "That could make a nice explosion."

In the meantime, Zafeer would become a legitimate businessman and make some money while he explored what it would cost to convince these stupid Mexicans to do whatever he wanted them to do. Recruiting them would be left to his subordinate.

Khalil Nadiman enlisted forty Mexican Nationals to unknowingly help them in their efforts to inflict damage to America. Khalil took care of all the small details. Just as he had since the group had been assigned together, he knew that his leader was carrying a personal jihad against America. It had been in his briefing at CIA headquarters. He had been schooled at Stanford University after his terrorist training in Afghanistan, but he converted to Christianity while in school and then contacted the CIA to become an undercover agent. His identity was known by only a select few in the intelligence agency, for fear of internal leaks. It was his intelligence that prevented the attack on the West Coast. He knew that if his leader ever found out, his death would be slow and agonizing and not the quick death he had just witnessed.

Back in the United States, a young woman in San Antonio, Texas, was crying out of control as she watched the horrible scene of the twin towers crumbling before her eyes. She thought of the unfinished lives that had been lost, the loved ones who would mourn forever at their loss. She thought of Pearl Harbor, but instead of a military invasion, this was an attack on an entirely civilian population. "Who would do this?" She thought to herself. "How many were just beginning to make sense of their lives, like me?" It was moments like this when she wished she had some family to talk to, someone who could be a voice of consolation and comfort. This wasn't the world that she was brought up in. Her world was something completely different.

While everyone from her graduating class had gone to college, Brittany Abbey had gone off and gotten married to the first boy to offer her a way out of the hell in which she lived. Her stepfather had been molesting her since she turned fourteen. Her mother, an expert in the art of denial and inebriation, pretended everything was normal by drinking herself to sleep each night, leaving her daughter at the hands of a sick, twisted pedophile.

Britt's marriage to Tom Abbey was doomed from the outset; she used him to escape her situation, nothing more. He must have sensed it, because it didn't take him long to start abusing Brittany with words at first, followed by the back of his hand and eventually his fist. Then one morning, Tom woke up to find a note on the refrigerator. It read: *Can't take the abuse anymore. Have a good life, you prick!*

She had bounced from one bad relationship to another after her marriage. By the time she was twenty-two years old, Britt had been molested, beaten, divorced, used, and abused, and was feeling quite lost. Life and some bad choices had shattered all her dreams.

Brittany had regretted not going to college, a decision she had decided to finally rectify after meeting a woman at a nail salon who made her take an introspective look at herself. The woman was in her fifties and was moving from one man to another, complaining about them and blaming them for her unhappiness. Britt saw herself in twenty-plus years and was appalled at her possible future, ran out to the local Barnes and Noble bookstore, and purchased some books on self-discovery and taking responsibility for one's life. She poured through the text, highlighted those things that definitely related to her, and took notes. By the time she had gone through each, she discovered that she was behaving like a victim, expecting to be treated badly, and then reacting accordingly.

"Oh my God!" She thought to herself. "I am going to be that pathetic woman in the nail salon. I don't think so. If I want to start over, I'm going to distance myself from my past. I'm not going to make the same mistakes over and over again."

Brittany went to the library, got online, and found a junior college that had a nursing program. It wasn't that far for her to travel, and it was a tourist town and a college town. Galveston was one of those cities that got a lot of visitors, and that was great for Brittany because her only experience was in the restaurant business. She was a beautiful blonde with gorgeous blue eyes and a perfect smile. She had enrolled at College of the Mainland, where she would have to take some brush-up classes and immediately put her name on the waiting list for their nursing program. Britt was used to waiting, but this time it would be different. She started filling out applications, and it didn't take her long before she landed a job at Landry's restaurant on The Strand, in the heart of the tourist district. "Galveston will be the place where I'll make my dreams come true." She said excitedly about her prospects. Brittany Abbey was elated with her fresh positive attitude, a new job, and college starting in a week. She would not allow herself to be a victim ever again.

Chapter Three: Blackouts

Michael was without emotion and speechless. Elizabeth was sure he didn't understand. So again she forced the words from her mouth.

"I have cancer, Mike. I will need to start chemotherapy right away."

He continued to look at his wife in disbelief. It was as if he didn't want the information to be true as she was speaking. His face contorted slightly, and Elle picked up that her husband understood.

"Mike, I need you to be on board with this." She was looking for reassurance. He finally found his voice and pretended to be okay.

"Don't worry, Elle, we'll lick this thing." He tried to be reassuring, but he had an anger building up inside, an anger directed at the only entity that had any control over the nightmare he and his wife were about to experience. He paced the floor at night, asking God why this was happening to them. When he exhausted himself of prayers, he would sit on the floor next to Elle's side of the bed and watch her as she slept. He wanted to memorize everything about her. All the while, his heart was breaking, and the God he had dedicated his life to was now going to punish him for the sins of the past. He couldn't wrap his finger around it, and the anger brewing inside was coming to a head.

Michael went to his church without the reverence he always had. The church was empty. He marched up close to the altar, his hands clenched.

"God, how could you let this happen?" Michael said out loud.

"After I changed my life, became the best person I could be, and devoted every free moment to doing your work. This is how you repay me? You're going to take my wife! You're an ungrateful God!" Michael screamed in the church he had been a part of for over thirty years.

"Why would you do this to her? She doesn't deserve this, you heartless bas-." He caught himself and fell to his knees, overwhelmed with rage.

"Where is the love you're supposed to have for your children?" He cried to the God he had loved so much, but that was coming to an end.

"I gave you everything." He said with tears in his eyes.

"I'm done doing for you, and giving to you, and loving you." He got back on his feet and shook his fists toward Heaven.

"I don't want you anymore. Do you hear me? We're done." With those words, Michael turned seething and walked out of the church.

He took a few steps and flashed back to himself on a bus returning to the base where he was going to be trained to kill. His decision to become a killer for his government was finalized in his young mind.

Upon arriving at the base, arrangements had been made for Private Angelino to depart for a secret training camp upon completion of basic training. He spent the next three months learning how to kill and how to survive the elements. The first four weeks were spent in a classroom discussing the human anatomy and all the different ways to cause death. Michael was an expert on the human body, but had never considered causing harm to it.

The next four weeks were spent in the field with a survivalist who taught the men how to eat almost anything and find water in the plant life of the jungles indigenous to Viet Nam. The final phase of his training was when many of the select group of men called it quits and were sent back to their units. It was a place Michael found the most peaceful. He was left for eight weeks with no food or water in a jungle similar to what he might encounter in Southeast Asia. This part of the training turned the young soldier into a deadly weapon, able to eat and drink to sustain himself on whatever he found in his environment, while fine-tuning his ability to kill. He was subjected to attempted attacks from his trainers. Each attempt sent the trainers running as they were shot repeatedly with rubber bullets from an expert with a rifle or beaten to the ground by a young soldier who had become everything they had hoped for in a killing weapon.

Michael graduated with no praise or fanfare. His reward was topographical maps of North and South Viet Nam, which he was required to memorize. Once locked into his photographic memory, Michael would imagine what it would be like to live off the land literally and to become an unseen force. He had learned to become one with his environment. He advanced with the breeze, allowing the sound of the thick foliage to camouflage his movement. His keen sense of hearing allowed him to detect which sounds were "normal" and which were alarms of potential danger.

He had become fascinated with the design of the P-38 can opener; its purpose was simple and effective. It was a device in which two pieces of metal were interlocked, and when placed in the locked position, could easily open a can. Thinking of the human anatomy, Michael contrived his own version of the device, one that was much more lethal. The contraption fit his finger much like a ring. It was a pointy, double-edged blade made of steel with a locking hinge to allow Michael to reach any of the major arteries in the human body.

His detailed knowledge of anatomy gave him a unique perspective on how to produce deadly results. He spent hours going over different scenarios that might occur and how his new weapon could be used effectively. It was something he didn't share with his trainers.

At night, he read out of the only two books he had brought with him, one was his Bible, and the other was about the military exploits of General William T. Sherman. He had memorized much of the Bible, in particular the story of Gideon.

> Early in the morning, Jerub-Baal (that is, Gideon) and all his men camped at the spring of Harod. The camp of Midian was north of them in the valley near the hill of Moreh. [2] The LORD said to Gideon, "You have too many men. I cannot deliver Midian into their hands, or Israel would boast against me, 'My own strength has saved me.' [3] Now announce to the army, 'Anyone who trembles with fear may turn back and leave Mount Gilead.'" So twenty-two thousand men left, while ten thousand remained.
>
> [4] But the LORD said to Gideon, "There are still too many men. Take them down to the water, and I will thin them out for you there. If I say, 'This one shall go with you,' he shall go; but if I say, 'This one shall not go with you,' he shall not go."
>
> [5] So Gideon took the men down to the water. There the LORD told him, "Separate those who lap the water with their tongues as a dog laps from those who kneel down to drink." [6] Three hundred of them drank from cupped hands, lapping like dogs. All the rest got down on their knees to drink.
>
> [7] The LORD said to Gideon, "With the three hundred men that lapped I will save you and give the Midianites into your hands.

Let all the others go home." [8] So Gideon sent the rest of the Israelites home but kept the three hundred, who took over the provisions and trumpets of the others.

Now the camp of Midian lay below him in the valley. [9] During that night the LORD said to Gideon, "Get up, go down against the camp, because I am going to give it into your hands. [10] If you are afraid to attack, go down to the camp with your servant Purah [11] and listen to what they are saying. Afterward, you will be encouraged to attack the camp." So he and Purah his servant went down to the outposts of the camp. [12] The Midianites, the Amalekites and all the other eastern peoples had settled in the valley, thick as locusts. Their camels could no more be counted than the sand on the seashore.

[13] Gideon arrived just as a man was telling a friend his dream. "I had a dream," he was saying. "A round loaf of barley bread came tumbling into the Midianite camp. It struck the tent with such force that the tent overturned and collapsed."

[14] His friend responded, "This can be nothing other than the sword of Gideon son of Joash, the Israelite. God has given the Midianites and the whole camp into his hands."

[15] When Gideon heard the dream and its interpretation, he bowed down and worshiped. He returned to the camp of Israel and called out, "Get up! The LORD has given the Midianite camp into your hands." [16] Dividing the three hundred men into three companies, he placed trumpets and empty jars in the hands of all of them, with torches inside.

[17] "Watch me," he told them. "Follow my lead. When I get to the edge of the camp, do exactly as I do. [18] When I and all who

are with me blow our trumpets, then from all around the camp blow yours and shout, 'For the LORD and for Gideon.'"

[19] Gideon and the hundred men with him reached the edge of the camp at the beginning of the middle watch, just after they had changed the guard. They blew their trumpets and broke the jars that were in their hands. [20] The three companies blew the trumpets and smashed the jars. Grasping the torches in their left hands and holding in their right hands the trumpets they were to blow, they shouted, "A sword for the LORD and for Gideon!" [21] While each man held his position around the camp, all the Midianites ran, crying out as they fled.

[22] When the three hundred trumpets sounded, the LORD caused the men throughout the camp to turn on each other with their swords. The army fled to Beth Shittah toward Zererah as far as the border of Abel Meholah near Tabbath. [23] Israelites from Naphtali, Asher and all Manasseh were called out, and they pursued the Midianites. [24] Gideon sent messengers throughout the hill country of Ephraim, saying, "Come down against the Midianites and seize the waters of the Jordan ahead of them as far as Beth Barah."

So all the men of Ephraim were called out and they seized the waters of the Jordan as far as Beth Barah. [25] They also captured two of the Midianite leaders, Oreb and Zeeb. They killed Oreb at the rock of Oreb, and Zeeb at the winepress of Zeeb. They pursued the Midianites and brought the heads of Oreb and Zeeb to Gideon, who was by the Jordan.

He understood that he must put his faith in God and trust that God would protect him.

Michael had always taken an interest in the Civil War, growing up near the town of Gettysburg, where the bloodiest three-day battle occurred. General Sherman's reasoning about war was a major reason the conflict ended as quickly as it did.

The General said. *"War is cruelty. There's no use trying to reform it. The crueler it is, the sooner it will be over. Every attempt to make war easy and safe will result in humiliation and disaster. My aim, then, was to whip the rebels, to humble their pride, to follow them to their inmost recesses, and make them fear and dread us. Fear is the beginning of wisdom."*

Michael began to make his own sense of what he had been asked to do, and although he was mortified at what he must do, his understanding of the savageness of war would work to his advantage. He thought to himself, "I will become the unseen, doing the unthinkable. I will bring my horror to the foot of their door, creating an uncontrollable fear that will make the enemy too cautious and too frightened, and it's just where I want them to be."

With the training over and orders in hand, Michael was dropped into the jungles of Viet Nam. His first assignment was the extermination of one-star General Taun Hoang, an American-educated Viet Cong. Hoang was a brutally merciless commander who had been responsible for a staggering number of U. S. casualties. His men had captured American soldiers and used severe torture measures in an effort to gather information about troop movement. Michael's instructions were clear: terminate the General, and they were purposefully unspecific. Michael had already come up with a game plan that, if successful, would cause tremendous fear in an already superstitious enemy.

He found himself in a remote area in northern South Vietnam in the province of Quan Tri, where the General's headquarters had been previously pinpointed. He examined the vegetation for food and water sources as he moved quietly through the thick undergrowth.

The monsoon season had begun, and the rain suddenly came down in buckets. He listened carefully to the pattern of sounds created by the rainfall. It had its own rhythm. Periodically, he stopped and listened, seeking the sounds that were out of place. His search for the inappropriate didn't take long.

He heard the sound of twigs breaking underfoot. Michael clicked his homemade weapon into position. He waited without movement, without breathing, as the sound moved closer. It was a lone combatant who would be his first example to his enemy that a nightmare had come to them. He watched as the soldier moved past him. His movement was swift as one hand went over the enemy's mouth and the make-shift silencer punctured the carotid artery in his neck. He gently brought down the corpse to the ground and made an incision into the enemy's chest. He was surprised after making his first cut into human flesh because steam suddenly rose from the soldier's body. He hadn't expected it. His only other experience had been cutting through cold beef hanging from a hook in his father's walk-in refrigerator. It looked like the soul was leaving the body. So Michael made the sign of the cross and continued the surgery. The next ten minutes were a careful dissection of a human corpse, as Michael removed the heart from the soldier and placed it in his right hand, and then removed the head and placed it in his left hand. He then positioned the body carefully into a cross. This was his way of sending a message to the enemy that God was coming for them. The heavy rain made the body temperature go down quickly, and it no longer created a steamy mist. He continued to move toward his ultimate target, which was still about five miles away. The new military hired gun encountered very little resistance. He repeated his ritual–like surgery two more times before he found himself just outside the enemy compound. Time was of the essence, as he had left a trail of death that, once discovered, would make the jungles come alive with movement.

He was thankful for the country's torrential rain, because it made it easier for him to move undetected under the multiplex of raised huts on the inside of the compound. He looked through the crudely made floorboards to see its occupants, and in a very short time, he found his objective. Once his target had been confirmed, Michael moved quickly. He crawled to the General's bed, his commando knife already pulled from its sheath. In one quick movement of his blade, the General's head disengaged. The only sounds were the gurgling of blood being pumped out of his carotid artery and the reflexive movement of his legs as his corpse continued to dance against the sheets. Michael began removing body parts with the same surgical precision, creating a scene of horror he was sure would traumatize the Viet Cong. He retraced his retreat into the darkness of the jungle night. Once back to a safe haven, the soldier fell to his knees and asked God to forgive him for what he had done and must continue to do for his country.

Days turned into months as the body count mounted. The results of his exploits were beginning to have a devastating effect on the enemy. Michael moved through the jungle like a panther, unseen and unrecognized by all except the few American soldiers who were spared their lives by his quick action.

In the blackness of night, two American voices could be heard discussing in whispered voices their R & R. As the lonely and tired men made hushed plans, a Viet Cong sniper began to zero in on their location. The North Vietnamese soldier raised his rifle. Suddenly, he heard a zipping noise and felt something touch his stomach. His eyes opened widely when he saw his intestines falling out of his body. In an instant, his head was jerked to the right, and the soldier fell to his death. His attacker dragged the enemy toward the infantrymen's location. He signaled his approach with a whistle, "Happy Easter, fellas!" He said as he dropped the body and disappeared into the black jungle. The two men who were saved recounted the story to other soldiers, who then passed it on until a legend had been born.

In the darkness of the jungle lived a soldier who killed viciously; he had become known by his enemy as *Docteur Fou*. *Docteur Fou* was French for *mad doctor*. The Viet Cong had picked up the French language during the late fifties French occupation of their country. His name brought absolute terror to the enemy, for they had no face or description to place on the phantom that killed with surgical precision and left their friends in pieces across the dense southeast jungle. Michael left some bodies mutilated almost beyond description. Sometimes he would skin them and leave the carcass hanging from a tree. When he used a rifle or pistol, he would put enough holes in the victim so as to avoid any confusion as to who had done the execution. Once Michael became aware of his nickname, he would leave a caduceus insignia patch at the site of his offense, which became another reminder of who was responsible, thus increasing the fear factor for the enemy. Michael understood war very well, and he made it very clear to the enemy that it wasn't pretty.

The U.S. Army and Marines had their own nickname for him. He became known as *The Machine*, a killer who never showed emotion, dissecting the enemy into pieces or firing his weapon until the corpse was beyond recognition. The Machine was racking up a body count and a reputation. Sergeant Michael Angelino had just turned twenty years old and had recorded his two hundredth kill in eighteen months. The device around his finger had become an integral part of his arsenal. He had become a master in the art of killing.

On the rare occasion when he worked in tandem with U.S. Forces, lives were spared by his undercover assault on the enemy. When the enemy came across one of their comrades who had become a victim of Michael's unique way of killing, they could not contain their fear. Screaming *"Docteur Fou,"* Viet Cong scrambled in every direction to get away from their own potential death, allowing seasoned U.S. forces to assault the retreating enemy.

Michael had made only a few friends while in the tropical forests of Viet Nam. One in particular was Sergeant Xavier Sanchez. Sanchez was a long-distance shooter who had confirmed kills from over three-quarters of a mile away. He was what was known as a shadow, backup for the primary assassin. His ability to read wind conditions and account for the movement of his target made him invaluable for long-distance extermination. A bit on the wild side, Xavier was famous for his drunken brawls with Marines. He had told Michael he hated the Marines taking all the credit for every successful military campaign. So it was not unusual to find Xavier in the stockade whenever he was not needed on the battlefield. Michael had nicknamed him "Excess."

There had been only one time when Michael was at death's door. He had attacked a pair of Viet Cong with his homemade blade as he had done numerous times before, but when he went to slash the throat of the second man, his weapon made contact with some kind of metal instead of flesh. It was the soldier's bayonet. The soldier turned quickly and swept Michael's feet, causing him to fall onto his back at the mercy of his enemy. Suddenly, he felt blood and brain matter splashed against his face, followed by the distant sound of rifle fire. His enemy fell forward right on top of Michael. The rifle fire continued for many minutes, and all around him, he heard bodies falling to the ground. He didn't move as more Viet Cong emerged from the shadows and then were dropped by someone with incredible aim. When the jungle was again quiet, Michael removed the corpse that covered him and found his way back to safety. It didn't take him long to find Excess.

"It was you, wasn't it?" Michael questioned.

"It looked like you could use a hand, amigo." The sharpshooter said jokingly as he finished his beer.

"I owe you, my friend." Michael almost smiled back at him. It would be the last time he saw Xavier Sanchez in Viet Nam. Michael had received orders to go home.

By the time Docteur Fou was decommissioned, he had been promoted to the position of Staff Sergeant E-6. He had received an array of medals, including four silver stars and nine bronze stars. Michael Angelino made his way to the military transport that would be bringing him home and received salutes and nods from soldiers who knew who he was and what he had done to save lives. Upon receiving his discharge from the Army, Michael found a sealed envelope with his discharge papers. It contained two letters; one a reference from General Andrew Goodpastor to the Federal Bureau of Investigation. In it, the General praised the young soldier for unfaltering dedication to his job and his ability to get the job done no matter what was asked of him. It was a recommendation that would not be ignored by anyone associated with the federal government. The other letter was handwritten by the President of the United States, thanking him for a job well done.

Michael had been unsure of his future after leaving Hell, but the letters he thought might be a way of securing a good life for him and the woman he loved. As he sat aboard the military transport, he prayed to God a prayer of thanks for sparing his life, followed by a prayer for forgiveness for the sins he had committed against his fellow man.

Upon his return, he married Elizabeth Carter, who got pregnant almost immediately after. He used the letters to secure a job with the FBI at first as a field agent in Mexico City, Colorado, and Los Angeles. Within five years, Michael was transferred to the Pentagon and worked his way through the ranks until he eventually held the position of Head of the terrorist activity task force.

Michael prayed every day for forgiveness. He was true to his word, making God a part of his everyday life. He had become the best man he could be, a good father to his son Joshua, a tactical asset to the FBI, and a true example of a Christian. He left the horrors of Viet Nam there on the battlefield and never mentioned what happened there to anyone except his Elizabeth. She went to school while he was doing field work and became a registered nurse. They settled in Gettysburg just a few minutes from the heart of the town. Michael had become the man he was meant to be, and almost everything was wonderful in his life.

The police car's lights were flashing as a loudspeaker asked the man on the sidewalk to please stop. The report read of a balding, gray-haired, bearded man missing for almost twenty hours.

"Sir, could you please show us some identification?" The young officer asked as he approached the man.

The man reached into his pocket and pulled out his wallet. He handed the whole wallet to the officer, a glazed look on his face. The officer saw the license and told his partner to call in that they had found Michael Angelino. The officer could see that the man was disoriented, so he helped him into the squad car and headed for the Gettysburg Hospital.

Elizabeth was already there when the police car pulled up. She had an orderly place her dazed husband on a gurney and transported him to bed nine of the emergency room. She tried to get him to respond, but he was in a trance-like state. The ER doctor had a CAT scan done of his head; it showed some minor swelling in the temporal lobe.

Michael suddenly looked up and asked, "What's going on here?" Elizabeth looked at him and could see the clarity had returned in his eyes.

"Welcome back, Mike." She said, relieved.

Michael was discharged within a short time, and Elizabeth drove him home. She had him sit on the couch and brought him a hot cup of coffee. He told her he was reliving his life in Viet Nam and not knowing where he was or what had happened during the lost time. It was information that only she was privileged to know. She sat stroking his face as she listened to him detail his Viet Nam experience, describing the reliving of his horrible past.

"I couldn't tell the doctor about it, Elle." He said, finally.

"Mike, the bump you got that day could be causing your blackouts, so for the next week, I'll be with you. No work. I'll call Tess and let her know we found you and that you're under doctor's orders for some time off. She'll be relieved." Elizabeth said in her nurse's voice.

"Elle, how long was I out of it?" Michael asked.

"Just over twenty-two hours." She remarked.

"Wow, that's a long time to be in another place and time." He said.

Elle kissed him on the lips, then said, "I need you with me, honey, especially now."

Chapter Four: Starting Over

There was no way to understand or really comprehend what was happening to Elizabeth. Each day, Michael could see a bit more of her disappear. The months that followed were hard, but she was so courageous. She coped with nausea almost every day after chemotherapy, with terrible, sporadic bouts of projectile vomiting. She tried to put on a strong front for Michael, who was driving back and forth from work, making the doctor's appointments and chemotherapy sessions. He was trying to be strong for her, but she could see him internalizing all his pain, not to mention the occasional episodes of lost time that she kept secret from his superiors. His heart was broken, and she knew he was very angry with God, but he needed his work.

Elizabeth began to lose her beautiful blond hair, slowly at first; then handfuls at a time. She had turned to wearing wigs and turbans at first, but she had come to grips with her disease, which was cancer, and nothing was really going to hide that fact. So out of sheer frustration, she took hair clippers and shaved her head bald. Michael returned home from work and found her crouched in the corner of their room, huddled into a ball, her hands over her newly shaved head, crying into her curled up legs. He knew she was incredibly upset, so he knelt down beside her. She knew he was there, but didn't lift her face.

"I like it." He said to her romantically.

"Liar!" She whimpered back at him.

"No, I mean it. You look sexy." He took her face in his hands and kissed her lips, still wet from her tears. She kissed him back. His lips felt so warm against hers.

"Have I told you lately that I'm the luckiest girl in the world?" She said through her tears.

He responded with a very corny voice and a silly cross-eyed expression. "No, I don't think so. No, I'm sure I would have remembered that." They both started laughing because he had never done anything like that before, and it surprised both of them. They couldn't stop laughing and didn't notice the young man standing in the doorway of their bedroom. He stood there smiling as he watched his parents in one of those moments of pure love.

"Are you kids making all that noise?" Joshua said jokingly.

"Josh!" In an instant, she realized she was bald. "Oh my God, I don't want you to see me like this." She screamed with embarrassment as she jumped up and ran to the bathroom. "I'll be right out, sweetheart." She yelled through the door. Josh went over to his father, who was still on the ground, and offered him a hand. Michael took his hand up. He was surprised when his son threw his arms around him and said, "I love you, Pop." Michael responded immediately, "I love you too, Josh." Somehow, the walls came down instantly, and the years of misunderstanding vanished in an embrace. Elizabeth came out of the bathroom with a towel around her head, wiping any tears that might still be exposed, and squeezed her son.

"How long will you be with us?" She asked excitedly as she embraced and kissed him.

"How long would you like me to stay?" He responded with a question.

"Are you kidding me?" She screamed with joy.

"Will someone answer a question, please?" Michael laughed. Then they all laughed.

"You must be hungry. Let me fix you something. I was going to do leftovers tonight, but this calls for something special." She went on excitedly as they all moved toward the kitchen. Elizabeth then slipped into the garage for something, while the men stood near the kitchen counter.

"Can you really stay for a while, son?" Michael asked sincerely. "I'm in the middle of this task force stuff, and I hate leaving your Mom."

"That's why I'm here, Dad. I know how important what you are doing is, and I thought if I could help you out, you wouldn't be feeling split in two. How is she doing, truly?" Josh questioned.

Michael responded, "She's getting weaker and thinner with each day that passes."

Elizabeth returned with three russet potatoes. "How does steak and baked potatoes sound?" She asked her men. "That sounds great, Mom," Joshua responded quickly. Michael nodded in agreement. With that, Elizabeth went to work in the kitchen, while the guys disappeared into Michael's office.

Elizabeth was beginning to worry as she was putting the last few platters of food on the table. "Boys!" she called out to them, but got no response. She went back into the kitchen to get the salt and pepper shakers. As she turned back around, she gasped loudly

64

because the men of her life were standing in the dining room, arm in arm with cleanly shaved heads. She began to cry and laugh at the same time. Michael and his son grabbed Elle and danced together in the kitchen. Joshua pulled the towel off his mother's head and swung it around, and then they put their three bald heads together. They were a happy family again.

Their happiness was short-lived, as the side effects of the third round of chemotherapy and radiation therapy were taking their toll on Elizabeth's ravaged body. Her weight had gone down even more; she was black and blue all over from falling down, caused by the numbness in her extremities, and she was having difficulty making it to the toilet on time. Michael did everything to make her comfortable, but kept getting called away.

She was mortified when her son had to change and clean her after soiling herself. Josh assured her with, "You changed me when I couldn't do it myself. So now it's my turn. It's no big deal, Mom."

Michael was gone on matters of national security, but his trips were getting shorter each time. Tess was trying to handle more and more of his workload so he could be with Elizabeth. He had trained Tess well, but there were still things that required his personal involvement, and it couldn't be avoided. In the meantime, Elle was losing her fight against the cancer, and Michael could sense that their time together was slipping away.

"Mike, they need you here in DC for at least 2 days," Tess announced when he answered the phone. He responded to her in a way he never had before. "Tell the fuckers I'll be there when I get there." Tess bit her lip nervously and said, "I'll tell them you'll be here as soon as you can, Mike. Is there anything I can do for you?" Her compassion brought him out of his anger.

"Thanks, Tess, sorry." They spoke for a while as she detailed to him what was going on. He needed to be in Washington, DC, as soon as possible to discuss pockets of terrorist activity that were discovered in Hawaii at the same time as the 9-11 attacks, and the CIA provided information from an unknown source that there was a cell moving into Mexico City that had made an attempt to blow up the Golden Gate Bridge. He needed to organize a special task force for the purpose of working with the CIA and exposing who these perpetrators were, and if possible, extracting them from Mexico City for interrogation. It would take him from his wife for only two days, two very precious days.

Elizabeth had been placed in a hospital bed by Hospice just a week before, as her condition was reaching the point of no return. Michael pulled out the lawn mower to cut the grass before he left for DC. Then he made his way up the stairs to say goodbye.

"Hey, Elle, are you awake?" He said softly, his head peeking through the door of their room. She looked up and smiled. "Come here, Mike." She answered weakly.

"I'm going to be out of town for a few days, Babe. Think you can keep things around here under control, while I'm gone?" He said, smiling down at her ravaged body. She nodded. Michael then pressed the button on her bed to raise her head. "I left you something. Look down at the lawn." He said softly. Elizabeth looked out her window and began to tear up. In the slightly overgrown lawn, Michael had written the words *I love you* with the lawnmower.

"I love you so much." She said as her soft hand touched his face. He took it in his hand and then softly kissed it, as a tear ran down his face. She took her finger and caught his tear, then placed the tear in her mouth. "I'll be back as soon as possible." He said as he kissed her lips, cheeks, and lips again.

Downstairs, Michael sat with his son, giving him instructions and going over her newest medications one more time.

"Don't worry, Dad, I got this. Just get back as soon as you can." Joshua assured his father.

Michael got his already packed suitcase and headed for his car. Joshua ran out of the house and embraced his father. Michael hugged him back. "I love you, Dad. I'm sorry I was such an asshole the past few years. I know what you're doing is important." Michael smiled at his son with pride over his newfound maturity. Then he said as he got into the car. "Well, it's not like I'm James Bond."

"That's for sure." Josh thought to himself as he watched his father drive away.

Later that night, Josh went in to feed his mother some chicken noodle soup with saltine crackers. His mother was just raising her bed when he entered the room. She said. "Josh, I need you to go into my hope chest and pull out the red album. It's at the very bottom of the chest." Josh did as he was told, and after a few minutes of digging through her things, pulled out the red album with the words Sgt. Michael Angelino.

"Josh, come sit with me." She said as she held the album close to her chest.

Her son moved next to her, curious about what she might show him. She began, "Your father loves us more than anything in the world. He also loves America and all it stands for. When your father was in Viet Nam, he wasn't in finance like he told you. He was much more." With that, she slowly opened up the album to a letter by the President of the United States. It was a handwritten thank you for a job well done. When Elizabeth turned the page, there was an award announcement for the Silver Star. It briefly described how Michael had put himself in harm's way to prevent his comrades from becoming victims of the war. Joshua finished reading the letter and turned the page to find another Silver Star proclamation. He began to cry as he read each page and kept turning pages to find that his father was a true American hero.

He turned to his mother and asked, "Why didn't he ever tell me about this?" She closed the book and again put it to her chest.

"Your father did things in those jungles that he said he would forever do penance for. He made a vow that because he was never wounded, he would devote his life to God and do what he could to bring others to the Almighty. Josh, he has tried to forget what he used to be, but it is something I think you needed to know."

Joshua took the album and replaced it in his mother's trunk, with a newfound respect for his father. He thought about what his father had said and then thought to himself, "Jeez, Dad, you are James Bond."

Moments later, the phone rang. Josh grabbed it. "Hello."

"Hey Josh, it's me. How is your mom?"

Josh answered. "I just lowered her head for the night."

"Son just put the phone to her ear." Joshua went into her room and placed the phone to her ear. Michael whispered, "I love you more than life, Elle."

Josh put the phone to his ear and said, "She smiled."

"Okay, love you, son. Thanks."

Josh responded, "I love you too, Pop," and shut off the phone.

Michael knew she was running out of time; it must have shown in his face as he hung up the phone. Suddenly, he felt arms gently embrace him from behind. He knew it was Tess, but was unable to contain his feelings. He turned to her and began to cry. She held him as he released his anguish. Her silent tears fell as the man she had loved for so long had already begun to mourn the loss of his wife. There were no words, and when he was able to stop crying, she released him and left the room. She was afraid to face him, angry with herself for having feelings for this man who was about to lose the love of his life.

Michael was losing it by the minute, but needed to focus as the conversation within the meeting room described in detail a plot to blow up the Golden Gate Bridge on 9-11. The intelligence appeared to be firsthand, and the information provided seemed to indicate a terrorist cell somewhere in Hawaii, but moving again, this time to Mexico City.

Michael asked point-blank, "Do we have someone on the inside?" The room was silent. He repeated himself. "Shit, is this a CIA operative?"

A suit from the far side of the table, a Mr. Stone, responded softly, "That information is classified."

Michael was getting angry with the politics, and said, "We just got our dicks whacked by terrorist forces, and you want to withhold information that might help us get them because you may or may not have a man on the inside. Does that make any sense at all?"

Mr. Stone said, "I am not authorized to provide information that might jeopardize our ongoing operation."

"Fine!" Michael replied. "If your man is there when we find them, he will not be recognized by this task force as anything but a terrorist. If violence occurs as a result, he may die."

Michael thought back to Viet Nam, when he was the only person to make a decision about life and death, and the only person he had to trust was himself. He knew he needed to be cooperative.

"Stone, get word to your operative that we will be moving personnel into that region. If he sees us getting close, he needs to extricate himself pronto." Michael said, remembering he was not alone in the jungle anymore, but part of a team.

He was already on the road home when a call came in from Joshua.

"Hey Son, how is Mom?"

"Not good," was his son's reply.

"I should be there very soon." Michael disconnected.

He was already off the freeway and on the country road heading toward Gettysburg. The commuters were already home for dinner, so he was making good time. He could see the light from her room as he pulled into the driveway. He jumped out of the car and made his way upstairs on the run. Josh was near the top of the stairs. His eyes were very red from crying, but he said to his father, "She's just waiting for you."

Michael peeked into the room and saw the love of his life; her eyes were open. She was waiting for her Michael. He put on their song. Tears began to run down her face as she smiled her best smile. Michael was also tearing up, but made a good attempt to sing to her as he moved closer to her bed.

"Stay for just a while, stay and let me look at you...been so long I hardly knew you standing in the door..."

Her eyes met his, and she giggled. Michael laughed and cried back at her, then leaned over her ravaged body and whispered in her ear. "Do you wanna dance?"

The hero soldier picked up his wife in his arms, tears flowing down his cheeks, and slowly danced around the room. He sang to her as he rocked her softly back and forth in his arms. He looked up as he sang, knowing that he would lose it if he looked at her.

"We danced until the night became a brand new day. Two lovers playing scenes from some romantic play, a September morning still can make me feel that way. September morn..."

Michael looked down. Somewhere in the middle of the song, Elizabeth Angelino departed. Michael began to cry loudly as he continued to hold on to his wife. Joshua stood by the door as his father danced in the middle of the room, unaware of anything but his love. He didn't want her to go yet, just a little more time, just one last kiss. His wailing had a rhythmic quality almost like a chant. Josh silently sobbed from the doorway.

After some time, Michael gently placed her on the hospital bed. He knelt down and kissed her hands over and over again. He felt his son's arm around his shoulders. He wiped his tears. He carefully covered her. She looked like she was sleeping when he left her there.

He and his son went downstairs, and Michael phoned the people at the hospice. They indicated they would be sending a vehicle. Michael and Joshua sat and held each other, both wracked with sadness. After some time, the doorbell rang. Two very kind mortuary men introduced themselves and indicated they would be taking Mrs. Angelino to the mortuary. Michael had the young men wait with their gurney. He went upstairs and dressed his wife in one of her favorite and most comfortable jogging outfits. He picked her up one last time and carried her down the stairs to the stretcher. Michael placed her on the portable bed, leaned down and kissed her cold lips.

He turned to the attendants and said, "Drive carefully and take good care of her."

His eyes filled with tears once again. Josh and Michael stood close to one another as the van drove off through the darkness, both knowing their life would never be the same again.

The funeral was beautiful, but Elle wasn't there. The home they had worked on together was just four walls holding too many memories for him. Michael was lost after Joshua headed back to Anaheim. He found himself spending more and more nights in Washington, D.C. Tess tried to keep him on track, but he had lost all interest in his job. Michael did what he did because it made Elizabeth proud of him. Without her, it was just a job. The blackouts continued, and Elle wasn't there to keep it a secret anymore.

Chet Avery, assistant to the FBI director, called Michael in for a heart-to-heart talk. He saw that his terrorist task force head was in very bad shape. He closed the door to his office and asked Michael to sit down.

"Mike, I want you to take a leave of absence. I believe with some rest and time to think, you will be a better agent." He said kindly.

Michael tried to refuse. "I really don't think that will be necessary, sir."

Chet replied, "Consider it an order, Mike. Sixty days with pay, and I want you to see that psychologist you saw after the attack. You're still having blackouts. We need you to be evaluated carefully before you can be medically released."

Michael answered. "I didn't think I'd had any, but honestly, I'm not sure, so if you tell me I have, I'll have to believe you and get checked out. I don't want to endanger anyone, that's for sure." Michael thought about his wife checking on him and asking him questions about time and place. Michael stood and shook hands with Mr. Avery.

"Thanks, Chet, I'll stay in touch."

Tess saw Michael going into his office and made her way there.

"So what's going on, Mike?" She asked as she sat in front of him.

"Looks like you'll be handling things for a while."

She looked at him curiously and asked, "How long will you be out?"

"Officially?" He questioned and then answered himself, "Sixty days for sure. Chet's worried about me."

"So am I!" Tess admitted.

"I'll be fine," Michael assured her.

"You really think I'm ready to handle all this?" She asked.

"Absolutely, Tess." He said with conviction.

"What will you do for sixty days?" She questioned her boss.

"There are a lot of loose ends at the house, clothes to the Goodwill, scrubs for her girlfriends, you know, stuff like that. Plus, Chet wants me to see the psychologist about the blackouts." He replied.

She looked lovingly into his eyes and said, "If you need anything, please call me. Okay?"

Michael was too numb to understand her meaning. Tess got up and kissed him on the cheek while holding his face with her hand. He could smell her perfume, and for an instant, he was aware of her tenderness. He took some of his things and left, dreading going home to an empty house, a house without his life.

Michael went to the psychologist twice a week. They talked about Elizabeth quite a bit, and his blackouts soon stopped completely. He was able to share many things with the doctor, about Josh, about his work, even about his anger at God. They discussed everything but his past. The doctor felt that through their dialog Michael had removed the need to retreat from life, and as a result, the blackouts were eliminated. He made himself available to Michael if he ever just needed to talk, and Michael thanked him for his time.

It was the fourth week of his forced leave when Michael received an interesting call from Gary Titich, an old friend from the Secret Service.

"Mike, it's Gary. I'm sorry for your loss, my friend."

Michael thanked him.

Gary explained why he was calling. "The reason for the call is a little self-serving. There is a position opening up here for the

Presidential advance team. It would be a feather in my cap to get someone with your experience to join our team."

Michael continued to listen as Gary described the job.

"It would mean a lot of traveling to different places. However, since 9-11, the lead time in each location has been extended. Some assignments could last as long as three months. It's mostly investigative work, checking out leads on anyone or any group who might have a beef with the President, examining the President's itinerary and knowing what's going on around where the President will be meeting or speaking, and assisting with where to put our people along his route. It would be a lot of traveling, but I thought all things considered, it might be just what you need right now."

"Sounds interesting. The doctors have cleared me. I haven't had a blackout for almost two weeks. They think it was stress-related. You know, because of Elle being sick and all." Michael responded to the phone.

Gary added, "I understand, Mike. By the way, I spoke to Tess about it. She said to call you, but I think she was a bit reluctant about losing you. Is something going on with you two?"

"No. We've been working together for a long time, and I really think she's a little insecure about being in charge." Michael reassured him.

"Well then, please give it some thought. It would be great to finally work with you, Mike." Gary said.

"I will, Gary, thanks for thinking of me. When would you need a response? I was planning a short trip out to the West Coast to visit my son." He queried.

"Tess said you were taking some much-needed time off. When you're close to going back, call me if you're interested. Fair enough?" Gary offered, hoping he had made his case.

"Okay, Gary, it sounds very interesting. Thanks for calling." There was a pause. "I'll call you."

Gary said goodbye. He turned to Chet Avery, who was in his office during the call. "He's interested."

Chet said. "I'll hate losing him, but let's face it, the guy is getting too old for all this shit."

Michael flew out to Ontario, California, rented a car and drove to visit Joshua. This would be his first trip. His work at the Pentagon and at church had always kept him too busy to make the journey. Elle had gone a few times without him. She would tell him every little aspect of the visit when she came home and suggested that the next time they should go together, but it never happened.

When his car pulled up in front of the beautifully designed building in beautiful downtown Irvine, Josh was standing in front waiting for his father. The two embraced and kissed as if they hadn't seen each other in a long time. Josh took his father by the arm and escorted him into the building he had designed. Michael could scarcely believe his son's attention to detail.

"Very impressive, son." He said proudly as they moved through the ingress.

The tour included all six levels and ended at the small restaurant back on the first floor. A table was already waiting for them, and the waiter pulled the seat for Josh's father. The waiter opened a napkin and laid it across Michael's lap. Michael smiled at his son and raised an eyebrow. The table had a basket of fresh sourdough rolls and two glasses of a California Cabernet waiting.

"Wow!" Michael exclaimed.

"Neat place." Josh said proudly, "The chef has worked under Wolfgang Puck."

"Your mother told me about his pumpkin ravioli. So I guess I don't need a menu."

The waiter came over, and Josh began ordering. "We'll have the Caprese salad, the Pumpkin Ravioli, a Bi-steak, and one Tiramisu with two spoons."

The waiter nodded, "Very good, sir."

Josh picked up his wine, smelled it, then raised it up and said, "Here's to Mom, who's probably looking down and smiling at us right now." Michael clinked glasses with his son and said, "Salute."

The two had a wonderful lunch together. They talked about Josh's mother, and Michael told his son some stories of their life before he came along.

"Your mother was very athletic," Michael mentioned.

"I didn't know that," Josh responded to the announcement.

"She had the track school record for the mile. Funny, whenever we raced, she would always let me catch her." Michael was looking into space as he was momentarily transported to another time. Michael brought himself back from where he had gone and told Josh that Tess sent her regards.

"I like her, Pop," Josh said, watching his father's face for any signs of his true feelings.

"I like her too, son. So stop looking at me that way.

"Hey, I'm just saying she is sure attentive to you," Josh added.

"She's a bit younger, don't you think?" Michael rationalized.

"Hell, Pop, at your age, I don't think age comes into the equation anymore," Josh reassured him.

Just then, the waiter showed up with a beautiful Tiramisu and two long ice teaspoons. Michael's eyes got big when it was placed carefully between the two of them. As they were eating dessert, Michael told his son that his mother always worried that he wouldn't find the right girl.

"Anybody you're interested in?" He asked his son.

"I have a girl, Amber. I've been seeing her for a while, but she's in med school, and I've seen very little of her this past year. She's doing rotations at different hospitals in Los Angeles. You know, pulling twenty-four-hour shifts, zero sleep, and making life and death decisions…quality health care." He said, laughing.

"Any chance to meet her before I go back?" His father asked.

"Not likely this trip, but when she's got some free time, we'll come out and see you," Josh suggested.

"I don't think I'll be home." He told his son.

"What do you mean?" Josh asked, puzzled.

Michael proceeded to tell his son about changing jobs. He told him about the offer to travel and be active again. Josh told him he thought it was a good idea. He went on to explain his extreme sadness every time he walked through the door of their home. Josh nodded in full understanding. He reached across the table as his father's emotions were beginning to show and held his hand. Michael curbed his feelings with one more bite of the luscious dessert.

"Let's get out of here. I want to show you some of the work I'm involved in right now."Josh announced to his father.

Michael was glad he changed the subject. It was too hard to think about Elizabeth, let alone talk about her. As he followed his son to the parking garage, he wondered when the pain would become tolerable. Josh clicked the alarm on his Lexus, and both men got in.

"Nice car," Michael told his son.

"Thanks, I'm leasing it at the suggestion of my accountant," Josh stated.

"That just means you're making great money, and you don't want to help pay my salary with it." Michael and Josh both started laughing as he pulled onto Jamboree Road.

"This road got its name from a Boy Scout annual Jamboree in 1956, but back then, it was just a dirt road. Now, Pop, you can't even get a condo for less than half a million."

"I can't believe it. I guess I'll keep the house in Gettysburg." Michael said, shaking his head in disbelief.

The two men spent an entire week together. Joshua took his father to downtown Los Angeles, where they enjoyed Olvera Street, and

Josh proved that for real Mexican food, they were at the right place. He then took his father to Disneyland. Michael had always heard about the park, but with Josh as his guide, he got to experience the magical land completely. Joshua finished the day by buying his father a pair of Mickey Mouse ears with his name sewn into the back. Michael surprised his son when he proudly put the ears on his head. The week ended all too quickly for both of them, with promises not to let so much time pass before the next visit.

Michael made his decision. He was about to embark on a new adventure. He was starting to get excited again. Upon arriving back in Gettysburg, he called Gary to let him know he was proud to become a part of the Secret Service team. This was just what the doctor ordered. A change in scenery would do him good, but his only big regret was leaving Tess.

He called her at work the following afternoon after returning home.

"Hi, stranger." He said.

Her voice crackled a bit when she said hello. Her feelings for him were getting stronger.

"It's just me. Guess you heard about the Secret Service position." Michael said.

"Yes, Gary called me. Sounds like you've made a decision. Tess remarked sadly.

"I think so, Tess. I can't stand being in that empty house." He admitted.

"Understood." She replied

"Hey, that means a promotion for you, and a raise." He said.

"Maybe not." She said as a matter of fact. "They've already posted the position on the internal website, and I haven't received a call from on high."

Michael tried to reassure her. "They have to do that. Standard policy to post all jobs. Don't worry."

"Okay, then I won't." She responded flatly.

"What's wrong? I can hear that something is wrong in your voice." He asked sincerely.

"I don't want to talk about it." She said insistently.

"Okay, I won't press. I called to ask you to have dinner with me tonight." He said in a very business-like manner. "It might be the last time I see you for a while."

Tess couldn't answer immediately. Her heart was racing. She began thinking whether enough time had passed for her to express her feelings.

"Are you still there?" He questioned the silent phone.

"Sorry, Mike. I was uh…my phone dropped. Sure, I'd love it. What time and where?" She stuttered.

"How about Ruth Chris Steak House in Connecticut around eight?" He suggested.

"That sounds wonderful, but I'll be coming straight from work. I'm trying to finish a report for tomorrow's briefing." She answered.

"That's great, I'll see you then." Mike hung up the phone.

Tess finished her report and looked at her wall clock and swore under her breath, "Seven thirty, Shit!" She realized she needed to get out of there soon if she didn't want to be late. Tess ran into the bathroom with her purse and quickly took off her blouse. She wet some paper towels with some water and a very small amount of the liquid soap, and then scrubbed under her arms. She disposed of them; then wet some more with just water to rinse the soap away. The last thing she wanted was to smell like a day at the office. She found some deodorant in her purse and gave herself a swipe under each arm. She pulled out her arsenal of makeup and redid her face. She finished putting on her red lipstick and then put a light coat of lip gloss. It made her lips shine in the light. She gave herself a last-minute check in the mirror. She took out her favorite perfume, sprayed it in the air, and walked through where she had sprayed. "That should be just enough." She thought to herself. She began to leave the bathroom when she realized she hadn't put her blouse back on. She rolled her eyes and shook her hands in an effort to calm down and buttoned up. Then she grabbed all her stuff, put it into her purse, and ran out the door. She ran down corridor C, caught the elevator, and then made her way to the exit. Security waved her a quick goodbye as she went through. With her keys in her hand, she beeped her door lock, started the car, and made her way to the restaurant. Most of the major traffic had already left the city, and she found herself at the valet parking just ten minutes past eight.

Mike was patiently waiting inside. When Tess walked through the door, still limping slightly from her 9/11 injury, Mike felt his stomach flip mildly. She looked more beautiful than he had ever noticed before. He kissed her cheek.

"Would you like a drink before we eat?"

"That would be great." She said. Inside her head, she was going to find the nerve to tell him how she felt about him. It had been over six months since Elizabeth passed. Tess shook her head; her mind was racing.

"How about an appetizer?" Michael asked.

"No thanks." She responded.

A cocktail waitress came by, and Tess ordered a Long Island Iced Tea. Michael ordered a glass of red wine.

"It must have been a hell of a day." He said, commenting on the drink she had ordered.

"You could say that." She sighed.

After about half an hour of waiting, they were escorted to a booth. Tess was feeling the drink, so she moved the conversation to a more personal level.

"How is Joshua doing?" She asked. Michael described his visit to California and Josh's architectural business. He avoided any mention of Elizabeth. So Tess took a large gulp of her cocktail and brought her up.

"How are you handling your loss?"

Michael looked at the beautiful woman across the table and said. "I'm getting through it okay, I guess." He was curious about the way the conversation was going

"I'm in love with you, Mike." She even surprised herself as the words passed through her lips. There was silence as Michael looked a bit surprised at her statement.

"I had never planned on telling you." She remarked and then continued before she lost her courage. "I could see how much you loved your wife. Then, after she was gone, I thought you needed to know that in this crazy world, there was someone who loved you and someone who still loves you." Michael continued to remain silent, watching Tess expose her heart. She went on talking as her cocktail had taken full effect, and she was on a roll. "Unless I am the worst judge at reading people, I got the sense you might have feelings for me too." Tess had put it all out there, and Mike knew it was a very hard thing for her to do. He took her hand in his and kissed it gently and lovingly.

"Tess, I have always had feelings for you. Sometimes I felt guilty about it, because it made me feel like I was cheating on my wife, but I never thought it would ever become realized. You were like a fantasy I could play out in my mind." He could see she was very disappointed.

"I've just taken a job that will have me out of D.C. most of the time, and I'm in no position to start up a relationship when I don't know where I'll be and for how long I'll be there." He continued. "If I were to fall for anyone in this entire world, Tess, it would be you, but I am going to need some more time." With that, Michael leaned over and softly kissed Tess on the lips. Her tears reached his lips. So he held her face with his large hands and used his thumbs to wipe her tears away. She didn't want to understand, but she did. Michael didn't want to stop kissing her either, but he did.

"At least we know how we feel about each other." She said, relieved.

The rest of the evening was filled with the casual conversation of two friends who knew that they might not be seeing each other for a while. They both laughed about the many good times they shared over the years. The restaurant was closing as they made their way to the door. They stood outside waiting as the valet returned with Tess's car. Michael embraced and kissed her again on the lips. It was a loving, warm kiss. Tess looked at him and then wiped his lips of any lipstick left behind. She smirked and rolled her eyes. She rolled down the passenger window after she got in the car.

"You better stay in touch, Mike." She said.

"Promise." He replied.

Michael waved and watched her drive away, ran his finger over his lips, and thought to himself, "We're not just friends anymore."

That night in his hotel room, Michael found himself pacing the floor while discussing the evening with his maker, "What is this all about? Are you trying to get me over Elizabeth? It's not going to happen, Lord, so just leave me the hell alone." The man who always spoke to God from his knees was walking through the hotel room, pointing his finger angrily at Heaven.

Chapter Five: Intersection

"You've all become too comfortable in America," Zafeer screamed into the phone.

"We are only doing what we were told to do." Dr. Rashad Naseem argued back.

"I want you to activate the rest of the cell in Galveston," Zafeer ordered.

"Salaam alaikum." The doctor uttered into the phone.

His superior responded in English. "There will be no peace." Then he hung up abruptly.

Rashad Naseem was a cardiologist at John Sealy Hospital, a major part of the University of Texas Medical Branch. John Sealy Hospital had been a home to Dr. Naseem for over 7 years, where he had developed quite a reputation for his expertise in the operating room, but also one for his fits of anger. He had married a nurse from the recovery room, Nancy Tilwell, and they had two children. She and the children knew firsthand how angry he could get.

As a young boy, Rashad had been sent to a terrorist training camp in the mountains of Afghanistan. There, he learned the art of killing, as well as being taught a perverted version of the Koran. He caught the eye of his trainers, who saw in him more than just a suicide bomber. So Rashad was sent to the best schools and eventually found his way into the United States for medical school, followed by a residency at Duke University Medical Center. He did a fellowship at Parkland Memorial in cardio-surgery, where he was then persuaded to move to Galveston by a visiting physician from the University of Texas.

He was required to maintain communication with his superiors within Al Qaeda. They instructed him as to their long-range plans, which were to establish a number of cells in the heartland of the United States. He would be their point man and would assist other cells in the accomplishment of their terrorist missions. He would answer only to his superiors in Saudi Arabia. Once he had established himself in the community, he assisted others from the organization to become a part of the Galveston landscape. Bijan Amir, a dentist from Ohio, was instructed to move to Galveston and become a part of the collection's southern cell. He, like Rashad, showed skills far beyond his ability to blow himself up, and Al Qaeda made use of this to put him into a position to assist and direct those less qualified within the group. Bijan loved the life he had achieved in the country he had been taught to hate as a youth. His life was very good and very different from the huts of his Iranian homeland. He was not looking forward to going back to the Middle East, even though this would one day be expected of him.

Rashad began sending his family to Bijan, which allowed them to communicate freely whenever information from their leaders was being transmitted. Such was the situation when the western part of the 9/11 attack became a poorly planned fiasco that was not realized. They had been a part of the southern attack on the port of Galveston, but were told to stand down when the Golden Gate Bridge failed to crumble. Their team, which included brothers Jamal and Feroz Habib, owners and operators of a Mercedes service station and repair shop on Broadway in Galveston, as well as four more men who operated a local convenience store on Ward Rd in Baytown.

The word had come down from Zafeer that the destruction of Galveston Bay was on again. It would be on the first anniversary of 9/11. By late March, things had already softened up on U. S. national defense. The press was showing how easy it was to get through security checkpoints, and the terrorists were taking notes, finding the local and national news media the best place to get information about the weakest links in the protection grid.

Michael Angelino had closed up his Gettysburg home and found himself in Arlington, Virginia, for orientation into the Secret Service. With his vast experience in the Bureau, he was moved through the orientation process with record speed. By April, he was given his first assignment. He and Gary Titich were going to Galveston to prepare for the President's trip scheduled two weeks after the 9/11 anniversary in New York. Michael found it interesting to be sharing information with the FBI and the CIA regarding anything, but he was pleased to have the opportunity to stay in touch with Tess, even if it was only on a professional level.

Tess's phone rang twice before she picked up. "Tess Lamia." She announced. His voice made her tickle in her stomach.

"Hey, you."

"Hi!" She purred through the line.

"Did you get any word on the promotion?" He inquired.

"I didn't get it." She announced.

"What?" He almost screamed into the phone.

"Yeah, the position went to one of Chet Avery's cronies, a fellow by the name of Ted Hobson, but he's not available to take the position until late September. So I'm working under Chet directly until the switch over. Hey, at least I still have my job. Chet has been replacing people all over the place." She informed her old boss.

"Wow!" He responded to the news. "I was calling to let you know I got my first assignment and I'm going to Galveston."

"Cool." She commented on his news.

"I'm calling for any new intelligence you have on the terrorist activity in the south." He informed her.

"Michael! You know more about what's going on in the country than I do." She exclaimed.

"I know, I just wanted to talk to you. How are you, Tess?" He asked.

"Missing you more than I want to!" She replied.

"How about as soon as I get some free time, we have that important second date?" He asked.

"What do you know about second dates? You haven't been on one in over thirty years!" She said, laughing.

"I've been reading a little about relationship stuff. It appears to be all very scientific these days." He said as they both laughed.

"Okay, what did it say?" She inquired.

"Apparently, we are supposed to advance physically as long as our internal lie detector has not been alarmed by information provided in the first encounter. Did we have a first encounter, because I didn't feel it if it happened, and if it did, I hope I was good enough for a second one?" He asked her, confused.

"I am so impressed. You really have been reading about relationships. I think I'm finally getting to you. Oh! By the way, the first encounter was just great." She said gleefully.

"That's good to know. Anyway, I've got a plane to catch. I'll be in touch. Bye for now." He said and then hung up. Tess spent the next five minutes dancing around her office watering her plants, but only as an excuse to really dance around the room. She hadn't felt so good about not getting a job in her entire life. Somewhere in the back of her mind, Tess was concerned that something wasn't right, but she was just too excited to think about it.

Brittany was just about to take a lunch break when two gentlemen in sports shirts and slacks came through the door of the restaurant. They were conversing back and forth, and the smaller of the two gave her a hand signal indicating there were two for lunch. She nodded. The taller balding man smiled at her and said, "Thanks so much..." Looking down at her name badge, he finished "Brittany."

"Would you gentlemen like to sit on the patio or inside?" She said, returning his smile.

"The patio would be wonderful."

She sat them just outside overlooking the Galveston Bay and said, "Welcome to Landry's. Your waitress will be with you shortly."

Gary Titich was talking about his last assignment in Los Angeles and the President's arrival for the Air Traffic Controllers' strike threat. "I never worked so hard in such a small amount of time. This project will be a lot less stressful. We have almost five months to investigate local hostiles and whack jobs."

Michael Angelino was sure that he would be very busy here, but for the moment, he wanted to just relax and enjoy a good meal. The men spoke of how they would pursue their investigation. It was decided that they would work alone and report back to each other anything suspicious at least once a week. Michael liked that, although he hadn't worked alone in quite some time. Michael would investigate known cells within the area because of his extensive knowledge of terrorists, and Gary would investigate information provided about individuals who had spoken out against the President or his views. This was Gary's forte as he had been doing this for over fifteen years. The conversation moved to leisure activities, and they agreed to get in some golf when they could. As the men left the restaurant, Michael leaned over to Brittany and said. "Great meal, I'll be back." She smiled sincerely and gave him a small wave.

That evening, three cars arrived at the convenience store on Ward Rd. in Baytown. Pirro and Nadir Piruz had just closed the exterior lights of their business when they heard a patterned knock on the back door of the building. Pirro yelled for Yasir to open it. Standing close by with his hand on a pistol was Taj Gholam; he was always a bit antsy when their meetings were to take place. Once opened, doctors Naseem and Amir entered, followed close behind by the Habib brothers. They all exchanged greetings and then sat. Naseem had been informed by his sources in the Middle East that the Mexican group led by Zafeer El-Amin would be directing the next assault on America. On the anniversary of 9/11, they would exact another devastating message to the American infidels who refused to heed their warning to leave the Middle East.

"Jamal, you and your brother will be transporting the device from just outside the desert border town of Zapata. Our Brothers in Mexico will be establishing diversions in both San Ygnacio and Falcon on the designated evening. This will leave a very small corridor through which the transfer will be made. Feroz, here is twenty thousand dollars." Rashad Naseem pulled a banded stack of U. S. currency from his briefcase and tossed it to him. "This is payment once the Mexicans have handed over the device. I want you to take Taj with you, because if there is any trouble with the Mexicans, you are instructed to kill them all."

Taj nodded at the brothers and then to Rashad.

"Once the device arrives at Bijan's dental office, he will wire the explosives. Pirro, Nadir, and Yasir will transport the bomb to the key locations that as of yet have not been provided. Our supervisors are determining the best location, and once found, they will be sending a courier to meet me with the final instructions. If, for some reason, the prime location cannot be reached, you are to go where I will instruct you to go and detonate the bomb. You three may need to sacrifice yourselves for this endeavor. Allah will bless you if this happens." Rashad ordered.

The men had learned years before never to argue with the decisions of their leaders, so there was little dialog after Rashad finished delivering the instructions. He closed his briefcase and began to leave when the button on the case came loose, and the briefcase reopened on the table. He reattached it, pressing firmly just as his beeper went off. It was the hospital. Rashad got into his black Mercedes and sped down the road. On the way, he thought about a multiple attack on the United States, which would include Galveston and Los Angeles in a magnificent one-two punch.

The other men embraced each other and then went their separate ways. Pirro and Nadir remained to lock up their business. They silently thought of their possible fate. Pirro spoke first.

"My brother, if we are limited in time, I want to live for a while. Get in the car."

"Where are we going, Pirro?" Nadir asked.

"The Royal Palace Gentleman's Club," Pirro answered.

By the time Rashad got home from his emergency at the hospital, it was three in the morning. His wife sat up in bed and asked. "Where have you been?"

He didn't like her tone, but answered calmly. "There was an emergency at the hospital."

"But you don't have call tonight, I checked the schedule." She challenged him. Suddenly, the back of his hand found her face. Then he scolded her. "Don't you ever question me about where I am or what I am doing; your job is to care for my children, nothing more. Do you understand?"

It wasn't the first time Nancy had been hit, but it was certainly the hardest. She sobbed loudly, rubbing her sore cheek as Rashad took off his clothes. He lay down to try and get a few hours of needed sleep. She smothered her head into the pillow so he couldn't hear her crying, for fear that the beating would start again.

Michael had been thinking about Elle telling him to lay off the pasta. He remembered other times when she would comment about his weight. It prompted him to begin a weight loss program. So he began each day with a brisk run during the cool early mornings. He knew what to do, and increasing his metabolism, he knew would speed up the process. He had enjoyed the light fare at Landry's, so Michael became a regular and confined his order to grilled chicken breast and a tossed salad with vinegar and oil, but more than the food, he enjoyed speaking with Brittany. By the end of the first month in Galveston, Michael and Britt, as he liked to call her, had become great friends. They would get together every Wednesday afternoon after her shift at the restaurant. Sometimes they would walk the Strand or find a quaint coffee shop and sit for hours, Michael providing fatherly advice and describing his son and how he thought they would be just right for each other. This oftentimes made Britt blush. Whenever Michael called Josh, he would mention the wonderful young lady he should meet. Josh was in the middle of a high-rise project in downtown Fullerton, designing a multilevel condominium for a very demanding client. Michael loved his son's success but thought that he worked way too hard.

"Your mother would be telling you to make sure you take some time for yourself."

Josh smiled and replied, "I hear her telling me to take it easy every day, Pop."

Michael added, "Me too, son, me too."

Britt was just finishing her lunch duties and had already gone over the dinner reservations with the manager. She made her way outside near the patio and caught a glimpse of Michael waving from the parking lot. She raised her arm when, suddenly, there was the unmistakable sound of gunfire. Britt's arm never made it to the wave as she dropped to the ground. Michael instinctively removed his revolver and crouched low to the ground. A black late-model Mercedes screeched around the corner, the rifle shaft still extended out the window. Michael fired, once, exploding the rear window. He could see the blood splatter, then dropped his eyes to the license plate, which read 437MMB. The car began to swerve to the left and the right, but disappeared around the corner as Michael ran to Brittany. She was gasping for breath, blood squirting out of the hole in her left chest. She had a pneumothorax, but the bullet fortunately didn't strike her heart. He knelt down by her and comforted her; the sounds of emergency responders were already close enough to hear. When the ambulance arrived, he yelled for them to get her in the rig and then began barking orders at the paramedic. "I need a chest tube."

The paramedic answered authoritatively. "Listen, officer, we'll be at the hospital in just a few minutes." The look on Michael's face changed, and his voice seemed different to the paramedic.

"Give me a chest tube, or I'll break your fucking neck. This girl isn't going to make it to the hospital in a few minutes because a left pneumothorax will put enough pressure against her heart that it will prevent the heart from beating effectively."

The paramedic handed him a tube, and Michael performed a perfect chest tube insertion. Air and blood quickly moved through the tube, and Brittany again had bilateral chest expansion. Her color improved almost instantly. The scary stranger didn't need to ask what was next. The young paramedic handed him a suture set, and Michael tied off the small tube to her skin.

The ambulance pulled into the emergency parking, and medical staff met them at the door of the vehicle. Michael followed her into a trauma bed area. He told the doctor she was a witness to a crime and needed to be admitted as a Jane Doe. The doctor could tell by the look on the man's face that he was dead serious. The doctor called for surgery, and moments later, an orderly and a nurse came down. Within minutes, a report was given, and Brittany was moved upstairs to undergo the removal of the bullet. Once she was taken, Michael walked outside of the Emergency Room and made a phone call to the local FBI informing them they would be moving the young girl as soon as she was stable and to have a team at the hospital standing by so the move could take place without delay. Michael knew that she was the target. What he didn't know was the why.

Tess received a call from the Galveston field office with information about the incident and instructions from an unidentified Secret Service agent. She instinctively picked up the phone and began dialing.

"Hello. How are you, Tess?" Michael calmly answered his phone.

"Mike, what's going on there?" She hadn't answered his question.

"Something happened to my young friend Brittany, but I must have blacked out during the ambulance ride because all I remember is being told that the young girl I brought in was stable, thanks to the chest tube I inserted, would be undergoing surgery to remove the bullet, and they said I had probably saved her life en route to the hospital. I started talking with the ER doc, and he said she would be stable to move if there were no complications in surgery. They would be putting her in a holding room with a nurse until the FBI arrived.

"I got the information a few minutes ago. When I heard Galveston, I figured you must have called. How are you feeling right now?" She asked very concerned.

"I'm okay, I guess, but I haven't spoken to Brittany yet. I'm hoping she can shed some light on this." Michael had concern in his voice, and Tess noticed.

"So, who is this girl, Mike?" She asked.

"I think I'm detecting some jealousy in your tone. The book says jealousy is not a good thing." He lectured her teasingly.

"Quit reading that damn book and just tell me what she is to you," Tess demanded.

"I think she would be just right for Joshua. I've been playing matchmaker. I met her when I first arrived, and she kind of looks at me as a father figure, something she has never really had. Put your mind to rest, Tess. I'm not much of a rover." He assured her.

"I know. I hate not seeing you every day. I miss you." She confessed.

"I miss you too. I haven't had anybody flirt with me in months." He admitted honestly, and then he quickly changed the subject.

"I'm going to try and find out what happened to Britt, and I'll get back to you." He said in his back-to-business voice that she knew all too well.

"Okay, the local team will be arriving at your location in a short time. I'll let them know you are running the show. Keep me in the loop, mister." She said with authority.

"Yes, ma'am." He answered and hung up.

Michael made his way to the recovery room. Once, there was a nurse who told him to have a seat.

"I just got a call from surgery, and they were just about finished. The patient should be here in just a few minutes." She said as she smiled at Michael. He sat down and stared at the walls, remembering how many hospital walls he had seen over the past year. Each time Elle was in for another chemo treatment, he would be directed to the waiting room, where all he could do was think about how much he hated those sterile hospital walls. He was reprieved from his thoughts as the gurney arrived. Brittany was intubated, which didn't surprise him. The nurse began taking vital signs as Brittany opened her eyes. Within about thirty minutes, the young patient was more alert and oriented to her surroundings. Michael was asked to step out of the room for a few minutes. Once he was out, the recovery specialist instructed her to take some deep breaths, and the tube would be removed. Her coaching was effective, and Brittany was extubated without a problem. She was placed on a nasal cannula at about four liters per minute. The nurse stuck her head out the door and said to Michael, "She's still a bit sleepy, but if you need to speak with her now, it would be alright."

Michael looked at her name tag. "Carol, there will be FBI men coming shortly. Please let me know when they arrive." Michael asked politely. She nodded and smiled and then sat down to chart her latest procedures and vital signs.

With that, Michael closed the curtain that surrounded the bed for a bit of privacy.

"Hey you, how are you feeling?" He said sweetly.

"Like a truck hit me on this side." She began to point to her left side but recoiled in pain.

"I need to ask you some questions, okay?" Michael began softly.

Britt nodded. Michael began to ask pointed questions about her assailant. Britt was hazy at first; then she began to remember an incident that struck her as odd last week. She started to remember. "A very well-dressed man came into the restaurant with a leather briefcase. I sat him down, and shortly after, he was met by another man. They looked foreign; you know, dark skin, dark hair. They spoke very quietly and stayed for about an hour. I was just sitting at another party as the man with the briefcase stood to leave. All of a sudden, his briefcase popped open, and all his papers fell on the floor. I bent over to help him, and he got very angry with me and told me to just get away. I couldn't help but notice the papers scattered on the floor. I probably should have mentioned it to you, but I was so busy that day and really didn't think too much about it."

Michael interjected. "What was on the papers, Britt?"

"It looked like plans with pictures of the bay and the oil refinery. Some of it was in a different language, so I couldn't understand all of what I was seeing, but the man gave me a look that could kill. It was the same kind of car today, but I didn't see him in it. Is this a terrorist thing, Mike?" She was beginning to put the pieces together, and so was Michael.

Just then, there was a knock at the door. Michael's hand went to his revolver; he pulled it from his holster under his suit coat and pointed it at the door.

"Come in," the nurse said calmly as she stood near the door. Michael's finger was ready to discharge as many rounds as were needed. The door opened, and familiar faces entered. Michael pulled the curtain.

"Hey Mike, Tess says you could use a hand here. What's up?" The face was Kyle O'Connor, a young FBI agent who had a real good reputation with the Bureau. The other was Michael Recco, an Italian whom Michael had oriented at the Pentagon a few years before.

"O'Connor and Recco, now there's a lethal combination, a Mick and a Pisano. Let's talk outside." Michael said, smiling, then turned to Brittany. "I'll be right back. Okay?" She just nodded.

Once outside in the corridor, Michael instructed the men that Brittany needed to be moved to a different place, and a report that she was pronounced dead after her arrival at the hospital had to be sent to the press. I want her sent to Orange County Children's Hospital in California. They indicated they understood and left to get things started. Michael went back into the room. He took out his cell phone and called Joshua. Michael told his son what had happened.

"What can I do, Pop?" Joshua asked.

"I was hoping you might be available to help Brittany once she was discharged from the hospital. She will be given a different name and history. She is going to be in the witness protection program." He informed his son while looking at her in her hospital bed.

"Sure, Pop, I'll do whatever I can," Josh assured his father.

Michael said, "I love you, son." Then he placed his phone back into his coat pocket and turned toward Brittany.

"It isn't often you get a second chance at life, but I'm giving you one. Now you can go back to school and get a good education in whatever field you want, paid for by the United States government. Your testimony when this finally finds its way to the courts will be crucial in making sure these animals are put away forever. Sound okay?" Michael saw her face light up.

"I'll take that as a yes." He said. He started for the door, turned back towards her, and said, "I'll see you and Josh as soon as I can. If nothing else, he'll be a great friend." He walked out quickly and blacked out.

When Michael became aware again, he was standing in the inside of his rented room. He looked around in shock at an arsenal of military weapons. Many were duplicates of the ones he used in Viet Nam. His eyes widened as he focused on something he never thought he would ever see again...it was his handmade killing device. He put it on his finger. Michael looked over and saw a journal on his bed. He went to it and began to read it. He apparently went back to Gettysburg. His handwritten notes showed an assassin's surveillance of targets and an answer to how long he was gone. His hand trembled as he became somewhat concerned about the loss of time. A moment later, his phone rang, and his partner, Gary, was yelling into the phone. "Damn it, Mike! Where have you been? We thought you were dead!"

"I'm okay; I wasn't feeling all that well, so I shut off the phone so I could just sleep it off." He lied.

"For three days?" Gary questioned with true concern. "Tess filled me in on the shooting at Landry's. Is the girl okay?"

"Yeah, she'll be alright, but it would appear the cell in Galveston has been activated," Michael informed his partner.

"No shit? Are we going after them?" Gary inquired with excitement.

"At this point, there are a few unknowns. I don't think we move in until all the bad guys have been identified." Sound okay?" He asked.

"You're the expert on this, so you take the lead. Just let me know what I can do, and for God's sake, stay in touch. By the way, I thought you said nothing was going on between you and Tess. She has been calling for any information on you and sounded like she was a complete wreck! Give the girl a call, will you?"

"I'll do it right now, thanks, Gary. Sorry about going silent." Michael hung up, then pressed his speed dial for Tess.

She looked down at her phone and saw Michael's name appear. She fumbled as she pressed the talk button.

"Michael Angelino here, checking in." He tried to be light-hearted about it, but it wasn't coming off too well.

"Please tell me something, Michael?" She wanted answers.

"I believe that an Al Qaeda cell has been activated here in Galveston. I've been running down leads. Recco and O'Connor are taking our potential witness out of here and transporting her to California."

"Mike, they left three days ago." She commented with concern. He hesitated, unsure of how to tell her what was going on, and then just decided to spell it out for her.

"Oh yeah, I'm having blackouts again. This one was for three days." He said honestly. "They seem to be getting longer." He added.

"You need to get to the doctor ASAP!" She ordered.

"They haven't found anything so far. How many pictures of my head do you want them to take?" He asked her, frustrated with his dilemma.

"It might be time to see the psychologist again." She mentioned gently.

"Yes. I might just have to do that." he was lying, and suddenly her Michael was no longer the one on the phone...

Tess stared at her phone because Michael's voice changed, and what he said next scared her to death.

"My next transmission will be after the completion of the mission."

The phone went dead. Tess went to the personnel department in the records section and pulled Michael's file. His history in the military was remarkable, but the Michael she had known for ten years was nothing like the person she was reading about. He was described as a man without emotion. This wasn't the man she had come to love, but that voice she just heard sure was. She read further, "Goes by the nickname, *The Machine*."

Chapter Six: Surveillance to Action

The Machine had been carefully watching the men on the list. He bugged the convenience store and found them to be quite talkative after the store closed. He had already obtained new names and at least four businesses that were fronts for what appeared to be a small contingency of terrorist Al Qaeda within the Galveston area. The biggest surprise was tracking down their leader. Dr. Rashad Naseem would have never come under his radar, except for his faulty briefcase. He was watching the Mercedes auto shop where the getaway car was being stashed. He observed through binoculars the doctor entering the establishment. At first, he thought he might be just another customer until his briefcase popped open the way Brittany had described the man at the restaurant. It was all the evidence he needed to add the good doctor to his hit list.

The American lifestyle has given all its targets bad habits. These imperfections in behavior would be used to facilitate his attack. Michael had found Bijan to be the weakest link in their chain. He determined that the dentist would be his informant. He would also be the first example of the hell that was to follow. The Machine was calculating a timetable for his attack on the enemy. Each step of the way needed to be meticulously planned. His surveillance of the good surgeon had uncovered a wife-beating narcissist who thought he was Allah's gift to medicine. He would never talk, so he must be the first to die. All the rest of the terrorists must be eliminated within a very short span of time, so none of those still alive would know that their comrades were already dead. He had been watching them without drawing suspicion. He was just another face in the crowd, blending into the scenery. He thought about how much Galveston was not like Viet Nam, but that he was able to accomplish the same result by just being an older man walking through town.

The Machine was ready. He had observed in detail the habits of his enemy. He knew how they behaved each day. They provided him with a blitzkrieg operational plan. He loaded the extra weapons into the trunk of his rental car and headed toward John Sealy Hospital.

He parked the new sedan in the hospital parking lot and made his way to Rashad's office. It was only one block from the hospital, and the doctor always made his way there after morning rounds to see his private patients. The machine timed the encounter to the second. First, he opened the killing device on his finger. The crosswalk was busy as it usually was with hospital and office workers making their way to local eating establishments for lunch. The Machine walked just left of the approaching doctor. He brushed up against him and drove the fine blade into the doctor's right femoral artery. The movement was swift and only appeared to be strangers accidentally bumping into each other in passing. The self-proclaimed medical giant took at least four more steps before looking down at his blood-soaked suit and then falling fatally to the ground. The Machine was confident of his kill and didn't bother to look back at the results of his encounter; already a block away, while a confused crowd stood over the remains of Dr. Rashad Naseem. The assassin thought to himself, "His wife won't have to worry about getting beaten again." He went for his rented vehicle and pulled out his 380 revolver, slipped it into his shoulder holster, and then got out his hunting knife. He started his engine and said under his breath, "Now that the head has been severed, it's time to eliminate the body."

The killing machine left nothing to chance. So when Cheryl Wilcox, the dental assistant for Doctor Bijan, got off the phone, she told her boss that her son had been taken to the office for misbehaving, and she had been instructed to get there as soon as possible. "We just have one new patient, a Mr. John Smith, left for today, and I already have his paperwork ready for him when he arrives."

"No problem, Cheryl. I can do it myself." Dr. Bijan Amir said kindly.

"Nothing to chance!" The assassin thought to himself. He had already called the school pretending to be Dr. Amir and instructed the school office to have his employee's son, David Wilcox, brought to the office because she was coming early to pick him up due to a family emergency. He waited just a moment, then called the dental office as the vice principal, John Parker, to let Cheryl know her son was in trouble. This would leave Dr. Amir alone, totally alone. He watched as Cheryl drove away and felt a bit saddened at the fact that tomorrow she would be unemployed. Then he walked across the street and entered the dental office.

Bijan Amir was standing behind the receptionist's area when he opened the door. "Mr. Smith?"

"Yes." Responded to the Machine as warmly as he could muster.

"I am Dr. Amir. My assistant had to leave early today, but she left your paperwork here for you to fill out, and I will go and get your room ready. Are you in a lot of pain?"

"Not really, but I imagine that will all change pretty soon." He replied jokingly. Bijan smiled and then headed for the exam room.

The dentist had just gone into the room to set up when the door opened. He started to speak, but was struck so hard on the head that it brought unconsciousness. When he woke, his arms and legs were tied down with electrical cords, and he was staring at the face of his patient, now standing over him with latex gloves on.

"What is going on?" The doctor demanded to know.

"It's time to tell me a story, Bijan. I am here for information about your plans to damage America. So let me be very clear how this is going to work."

With that said, he pulled out a survival knife and quickly cut off the doctor's little finger. The knife was very sharp, and it cut quickly through flesh and bone. The dentist began to scream in horror, but was muffled by a wad of paper towels that were shoved into his open mouth. Bijan had never been trained to withstand this type of torturous interrogation and could not imagine the weak American government ever condoning this form of examination. His mind was trying to understand what was happening to him, but his finger was detached even faster. The unknown inquisitor then removed the towels from his mouth.

Bijan asked, "Who are you?" There was no answer, just another swift movement of the blade against the next finger, followed by the towels shoved into his screaming mouth.

"I ask the questions. Your job is to answer them fully. If I think you're lying, you will lose another finger. If you hesitate, you will lose a finger. If I don't believe you, you will lose a finger. I have been bugging you and your friends from the auto shop and the convenience store for a week now. So paint me a picture, Doctor Amir, and leave nothing out. Who is in charge of this cell?" The questioner without a name asked with firm authority. The answer didn't come fast enough, and the blade removed the dentist's middle finger.

He screamed, "El Amin! El Amin! El Amin!"

"Where can I find him?" The Machine asked quickly. The answers came just as fast. "Four Seasons, Mexico City!"

"How many are there?"

"I don't know," He responded as he had been trained to do so. The blade began to descend on another digit when Bijan screamed out.

"Many he has many men."

"What are your plans?" The madman asked.

"Originally, we were to blow up Galveston Bay and all the oil tankers docked there, but your news media told us the President was coming here. We received additional orders...find out where the President would be staying so that the people coming could blow up your President Bush and then blow up the bay."

"Anything else?" The cold voice asked.

Bijan begged for mercy. "I know nothing else, I swear to Allah! Please, I have a family."

The response to his plea became clear. The soldier with the knife looked the jihadist right in the eye. "On 9/11, innocent civilians were working hard so they could go home to their families. That day they lost their life. Today, Bijan, you will lose yours." With that, The Machine, whose face was just inches from the dentist's, took his blade and slowly ran it through the soft tissue of the enemy's neck. The screaming came to a stop as the blade moved through his vocal cords. Bijan remained alert long enough to see his own blood squirt onto the face of his executioner. The blade continued until his head fell to the ground.

He quickly began his ritual of surgically removing Bijan's body parts. The warrior from Viet Nam was back, and he would exact pain against his enemy and fill them with a fear they could never imagine.

The dentist's heart was placed in his undamaged left hand, and his head was placed in his lap, face down. He wanted it to be humiliating. He wanted it to be gruesome. He wanted his message to be heard very loud and very clear. Death was coming to those who fucked with America, and he would be its avenging angel. He pulled a mass card out of his pocket and placed it face up in Bijan's mutilated right hand; on it was a picture of Michael the Archangel. He went to the sink, washed the blood off his face, and then walked out the door. "Message sent."

The Machine had a short fourteen hours to reduce the terrorist forces before Bijan was discovered. He had made extensive notes about where his targets were and when best to eliminate them. His next stop was the Mercedes auto shop. Jamal and Feroz Habib had bought the facility five years before. They were trained auto mechanics specializing in luxury cars, which meant that they had many clients in local politics. The assassin used that information. He hotwired a late-model Mercedes sedan and drove to their business. He watched from across the street, checking his watch as the open sign was flipped over to the closed side. "Great timing." He thought to himself. He pulled out a three eighty with a silencer and placed it in his pants. He pulled up to the garage entrance, stepped out, and tapped on the office window.

"We are closed!" A voice from inside, speaking loudly with a Middle Eastern accent, said.

"Bo Quiroga sent me over."The Machine used his most friendly voice.

Suddenly, a face appeared in the window. He eyed the gray-bearded stranger.

"Feroz, the mayor sent this old man over to get his car checked." The face in the window yelled over his shoulder.

A second man appeared, just coming out of the bathroom. He buckled his belt, then went and bent over behind his desk.

"Tell him we'd be happy to take a quick look, Jamal."

Brother Jamal looked down, and the assassin could hear the keys jingling in his hand. He gently pulled out his weapon.

Jamal said, "We'll give it a look-see, but you might have to bring it back again tomorrow."

He was allowed to finish his sentence before the bullet from the 380 sent a direct message to the man's brain. It splattered his approaching partner with blood and brain matter. The gun sputtered again as two bullets exploded Feroz's heart, ending his life. The killer took the keys from Jamal's dead hand and replaced them with a mass card. Unexpectedly, he caught a glimpse of a man running through the back of the garage. He had one arm in a sling. The 380 fired a quiet round into the wounded arm, and the man screamed and hit the ground. The Machine watched as the man struggled with all his will to crawl away from the attack. The weapon fired again, this time tearing through his good arm. He turned, lying on his back, covering his face, awaiting death. He would not be disappointed.

Michael knew this was the son of a bitch who had shot Brittany.

The weapon fired again and again, each time missing any vital parts. The screaming was reduced to a whimper. The Machine emptied his clip, reloaded, and emptied another. He watched as the extensive blood loss caused the heart to be ineffective, and eventually it came to a stop. Michael went back to the office and found a safe ajar behind the desk. He removed two revolvers and over twenty thousand in cash. He locked the door and deadbolt, and then threw the keys over the fence near some parked cars.

In the meantime, Gary had tried to make contact with Michael but was unsuccessful. He decided not to wait another three days to call Tess. The phone rang twice.

"Tess Lamia, may I help you?"

"It's Gary Titich, Tess. I'm calling about Mike."

"Is he alright?" She asked, distressed.

"I don't know. He's AWOL again. I've tried reaching him, and nothing." He replied.

"Our office just received information about a doctor Naseem who bled to death a block from his office in the middle of the street," Tess informed him.

"Holy cow! That's one of the guys Mike has been following leads on." Gary blurted back to her.

"I'm going to see about coming out there. If you hear from him, call me immediately, okay?" Gary assured her he would.

111

Tess went into Chet Emory's office. He had just hung up the phone. "What's up, Tess?" He said, seeing concern in her face.

"A girl was shot, and Mike contacted O'Connor and Recco to have her placed into witness protection. A doctor, Rashad Naseem, whom Mike was investigating, died in the streets of Galveston this morning, and now Mike is missing. I'd like to take a team and get down there as soon as possible." She answered.

"Do you think people are in danger?" Chet asked her.

"I think the entire state of Texas could be in danger!" She exclaimed in hushed tones.

"Put your team together and get going!" Chet told her.

The Machine had been watching the convenience store for almost three hours when a car drove up with two more Jihadist soldiers. He calculated to himself, "That makes six." The place had no customers, and it was almost closing time. He thought to himself, "Time for action." He carefully checked his weapons, two shoulder holsters, one with his 380, the other was a 44 magnum, which he thought might be perfect if he needed to shoot someone around the corner of the store or behind a shelf.

The door opened, and the men inside paid little attention to the old bearded businessman. He went to the back of the store, where the cold drinks were kept, and pulled out two liters of Dr. Pepper. He was marking his targets for a clean sweep. He had a five-dollar bill in his right hand and the two bottles in his left. He dropped the five on the counter and waited for change. He took the change and said in his kindest voice, "Thank you."

He turned to walk out, took two steps, and let one of the bottles fall to the floor, then the other. The Middle Eastern men smirked at first, but their smirks turned to shock as the old man turned suddenly with guns blazing. Pirro, Nadir, and Yasir stood motionless as the 380 made large holes in their heads. The other three were scrambling to find anything they could hide behind. The .44 Magnum roared as it tore through shelving and flesh in the same instant. One of the soldiers had gotten a weapon out as he hid around the corner near the bathroom. The magnum fired through the wall, and the man's body dropped motionless to the tiled floor. The last soldier fell to his knees, begging for mercy. He had wet himself and was sobbing. The Machine thought for a moment of the tactical advantage of keeping one soldier alive, and then he thought of the innocents jumping from the twin towers to certain death to escape the flames that engulfed them. He looked down on the pitiful Jihadist and shot him in the kneecap. "Do you remember how happy you were when the towers came down?" Michael took his time, watched the enemy's face, then pointed his weapon at the other leg, pulled the trigger, and shot the other kneecap off with the .44 Magnum. "You're not so happy now!" The terrorist cried out in agony. The Machine ended the screams with four more rounds of the magnum exploding into the radical's face and chest. The Viet Nam veteran stood over the enemy's body and dropped a mass card into what was left of his face. He was splattered with the enemy's blood, so he went to the bathroom and washed his face. When he came out, he noticed a door open in the back office area. Once inside, he discovered a cache of money in a box just beside a safe. The enemy had again supplied his war effort with their carelessness. He took the whole box. As he passed the fuse box for the building, he opened it and turned off the main breaker. All the lights went out.

Chapter Seven: A Moment to Breathe

Michael had just unlocked the door to his rental in Galveston when the memory of the past twelve hours came rushing into his consciousness. He sat on the bed and began to cry bitterly over the resurrection of the monster he had been during the war in Southeast Asia. He had prayed that the assassin the government had unleashed so many years ago would be gone forever. The Machine had done what the authorities could not do to prevent the death of his President and the destruction of the oil refineries in Galveston. He thought seriously about the entire episode. This enemy had no rules of engagement; they had killed innocents, and they were trying to inflict damage to the very psyche of the American people. He recalled his meeting with the General when he was first approached.

"You will be a government assassin, but if caught, we will put out information that you were AWOL from your designated unit and that your actions were those of a mentally ill soldier who could not handle the stresses of battle. You would not be afforded any assistance from the government you work for, but make no mistake about it, Michael, if you agree to this assignment, you will, in fact, be saving lives."

Forever the strategist, he had only two choices: one was to turn himself in to the local authorities; the other was to continue the fight and somehow become an invisible phantom, much like the one he created during the Viet Nam crisis. Michael chose the latter, seeing no advantage to a life behind bars, but in order for this to happen, he must kill Michael Angelino. The political views he elicited when his alter ego had escaped, from deep inside himself, were not that far from Michael's own feelings when it came to terrorism. He was sure these men were cowards and a blemish in the eyes of true Muslims, but more than that, they were a cancer that was spreading their poison across the globe and making all peace-loving people shudder in fear. These pitiful specimens of rotting flesh had brought the war to everyone, everywhere, and that meant that no one was safe.

Michael wrote a message to Gary related to his surveillance. It detailed a rogue jihadist who had gone off the deep end and was responsible for the massacre that had occurred. He relayed to his friend that he was to meet a low-level informant named Punjab, who was going to provide him with information about an overseas connection. This was, of course, pure fabrication, but necessary to eliminate him from the equation. His other problem was to get documents made under an assumed name so that he could travel unnoticed by authorities and the enemy he was now after. He had a source in Dallas who was famous for forged documents and owed Michael a favor or three.

Michael, who was now considered AWOL, placed his wallet and some hair fibers in the rental car he was using. Took it to a remote location and blew the car up beyond recognition. The fragments discovered would provide just enough to convince the authorities that Michael Angelino was dead. The note was discovered by Titich the morning after the explosion. The personal belongings discovered at the scene of the demolition were enough to suggest that Michael was in the car at the time. This and a change in his appearance would give Michael a moment to regroup and decide what his next move would be, and he needed a few precious moments to think.

He had been losing weight quite rapidly of late, and shaving his head bald gave him the appearance of a man at least ten to fifteen years younger. The beard he had since entering the FBI was replaced with a small goatee, which he dyed from gray to dark brown. He added a pair of sunglasses, and the man in the mirror could have been almost anyone but him.

He needed to get to Dallas to get new papers and then a flight to Mexico City. Michael hotwired a car and set out to meet a forger by the name of Ken Kou. Kou had done a three-year stint in a federal prison in Miami when Michael first met him. Through some very persuasive meetings with Kou, Michael was able to apprehend two pedophiles who had been working together throughout the south. Michael was able to get Ken's parole moved up, and he had promised Michael his loyalty forever. For most people, that might just be words, but for a Chinese man, it was a question of honor and responsibility.

Kou didn't recognize the man behind the glasses until he heard his voice. He got up and embraced the man who secured his freedom. He disengaged, took another look, and then embraced Michael again.

"What brings you to Texas, Michael?" Ken asked with a smile.

"I need papers," Michael stated.

"You know I don't do that anymore." Ken lied.

"I will need multiple names, passports, driver's licenses, at least five or six," Michael told the forger.

"You must be in a lot of trouble, old friend," Ken said, watching Michael's eyes for a sign.

"You will never know my friend...and you don't want to. Understand?" Michael stared at Ken.

"You were never here. Got it." He answered.

Ken took Michael into the back room and took a number of pictures of him for the false documents. He had him change shirts, wear glasses, and even put him in a wig for one of the identities. He told Michael to come back in a few hours, and it would be done.

He stepped outside the building in the strip mall and made a call to his old Mexican friend Edmundo Moreno. Edmundo had been a CIA operative during the 1960s, and worked with Michael when Gilberto Guevara Niebla, a young radical student influenced by Chet, led the Mexican student uprising of 1968. The insurrection ended in a massacre by the Mexican army in October of that year. Michael and Edmundo had remained friends through the years. Edmundo had recently retired from the CIA for health reasons.

After some brief pleasantries, Michael filled his old friend in on what was happening. He explained that he was no longer with any government organization and that what he was doing could be a danger to anyone who helped him.

"When will you be here?" The old CIA agent asked.

"It could be dangerous for you," Michael assured his friend.

"I am an old man who sometimes can't remember where I live. No one places much value on anything I say anymore." Edmundo said sadly.

"The enemy I'm after has taken residence in your capital city, and I'm coming to kill every last one of them...or die trying."

"I shall await your arrival, old friend," Edmundo said and then hung up.

Michael went back in, and Ken was placing the documents in a manila envelope. Ken handed the packet to Michael, and Michael slipped him a thousand dollars of the enemy's money.

"Boy, you must be in some kind of trouble," Kou said.

"Save the pictures in case I need more documents," Michael told the forger.

"Anything for you, Mike," Ken said, then shook his hand, and Michael was out the door.

Tess received the news from Titich that Michael's revolver and wallet were found in his exploded rental car. She held in her emotions, thanked him for calling, and calmly hung up the phone. She thought to herself, "It just couldn't be." She wanted to be completely sure before she fell completely apart. She called Chet and told him she was going to get a connecting flight to Houston when her plane landed in Dallas to get updates from her operatives in Galveston. Chet gave her the green light. She immediately contacted the Dulles Airport for a flight out the next morning. Her head was reeling as she kept debating with herself that her old boss couldn't be fooled into being blown up, but perhaps an old assassin might be able to be tricked. She packed herself an overnight bag and dropped off to sleep, still weighing the facts.

Her flight arrived at the Dallas-Fort Worth airport at one in the afternoon. She had a distressed look on her face and a furrowed brow. Her cell phone rang twice before she answered. "Lamia here."

"I can see that," Michael said, smiling. Her eyes lit up.

"Where are you?" She said as she looked around.

"Get rid of the crowd." He told her.

Tess turned to her agents and gave them instructions to go ahead to Houston, and she would follow as soon as possible. They nodded and headed for their connecting flight to Houston. She put the phone to her ear again and asked, somewhat confused, "What's going on?"

"There's a lot to tell you and very little time. Look to your left." He instructed her. As she looked, she saw a bald man in dark sunglasses waving at her.

"I love the new look, no wonder everyone thinks you're dead." Michael's look changed quickly to grim. Tess couldn't help but giggle over his look and the fact that he was still alive. She ensured that her team was gone and then went over to him and rubbed the top of his head.

They walked out of the airport arm in arm and went to the car Michael had hotwired the night before in Galveston.

"Tess, Michael is dead." He whispered under his breath. His look was very grim. Tess immediately understood.

"The report of terrorists dead and mutilated, that was you, wasn't it?" Tess inquired, afraid that she was right.

"It was going on during a blackout," Michael answered her.

"I only became aware of what happened a day ago. If I turn myself in, I appear like a paranoid vigilante, and the press would have a field day with me. You know my history. It would all come back to haunt me. In the meantime, real terrorists would be able to move forward during the circus and do more damage to our country.

I can't let that ever take place. Someone has to bring the war to them, and it would seem this old fart is the guy to do it."

Tess just stared at him as he pulled into a motel parking space quite a distance from the airport. She wasn't sure what to say or how to say it.

"Could you use a bite to eat?" His question took her out of her trance.

"That would be great." She answered, still trying to take in his new appearance.

"It makes you look younger, you know."

"Thanks, I wouldn't appear much of a threat with my gray beard and protruding stomach." He said, smiling at her.

The diner was almost empty when they walked in. Michael scanned the room. A waitress appeared from out of the kitchen area and told them to sit anywhere. Michael directed them to a place facing the door. He was carrying his favorite weapon, the 380 with a silencer in place in his shoulder holster and two extra clips in his pocket. He was in his war mode, and he was ready for anything.

Tess was still looking for words, and her beautiful blue eyes were on the verge of tears as she stared at the man she loved for so many years. He recognized her look and answered her before the question formed on her lips.

"My destiny has changed, Tess. You shouldn't wait for me. I may not be here that long." His implication made the tears fall from her eyes.

"What can I get you folks?" The waitress asked as she approached the booth.

Tess wiped her eyes and asked for a cup of coffee. Michael asked for the same. The waitress left for a moment and returned with a fresh pot. She flipped the heavy mugs over and filled each.

"Are you ready to order?" She asked as she finished pouring.

"Give us a few minutes," Michael answered, all the while looking at Tess. The waitress walked away, leaving the two friends to talk for a while.

Tess picked up the conversation where it left off. "Were you planning on dying soon?"

"Never know about things like that, but the odds don't look that great for survival, but they are better than I've had before." He was recalling Viet Nam. He went on.

"Their biggest problem is they are in my world right now; that works in my favor. I'm not a zealot with an emotional justification for killing; that would make me sloppy. I'm a trained assassin. My job is to kill them and keep killing them until they are all dead; that makes me dangerous."

"What about us?" She already knew the answer. Michael didn't answer her. Instead, he opened the laminated dinner menu and told her to order something.

The conversation was limited to dinner and small talk until they left. As they walked toward the motel, Tess wanted to know in detail what had gone down the day before she arrived. Michael gave her every detail and his reasoning behind it. He knew she understood war from their numerous conversations about the civil conflict between the states.

She told him, "I can be a great inside source; you'll need information."

"I don't want you involved." He said harshly.

She snapped back. "It's too late for that!"

He unlocked the door to the motel room, and they went inside. It was dark except for the flashing neon light from the motel sign outside the second-story window. It was a hot, sweltering Texas night as she moved close to him in the darkness. He could feel her moist skin and smell her perfume as it melted off her long neck. Michael had waited so long to hold Tess that he almost didn't know where to start, but his experience in the art of lovemaking was extensive, even though it was limited to only one. He carefully began his exploration of her. Tess's lips were soft and moist as he ran his tongue across them, followed by hot, passionate kisses moving over her face. His passion soon became unbridled, biting her lips. She winced from the pain and then bit him back. They were both experiencing so many emotions. He wanted to consume her after so many years of fantasizing about how she might be as a lover. He moved his lips down her neck, like an animal bearing his teeth, gently biting and kissing her neck over and over. Suddenly, she began to lose control. With each passionate taste, her moans filled his ears and filled the room. Tess had loved Michael for years, and in an instant, nothing existed but his touch. He slowly unbuttoned her white cotton blouse, then peeled off her delicate bra from her damp skin, exposing two beautiful breasts with pink nipples, erect and waiting, wanting to be touched. His fingers found their way to them and gently massaged the contours of their fullness, his fingertips finding her nipples and pinching and pulling gently until he could bring his mouth to them. He bathed each breast with soft wet kisses, back and forth, one side to the other, sucking each with equal attention. Watching Tess's face as her eyes closed and opened with each movement of his lips, her mouth uttering sounds without meaning. They somehow found the bed. Tess found herself lying back against the sheets, as Michael moved his attention south, kissing and licking his way past her navel to that place reserved for lovers. Once there, Michael stared up at her for a response. Tess had moved into a state where nothing mattered but the touch. She tasted like honey, so he explored her sweetness with his tongue, softly kissing the essence of her, revisiting each inch of her until he could recognize it by touch, and with each touch, she quivered. Michael took pleasure in her satisfaction, as he brought her to conclusion, patiently waited for her recovery, then made her peak again. Tess's inner thigh began to twitch with spasm. Michael recognized her need to feel him inside her. His hands moved over her body, feeling cold sweat on a body so warm, so hot, that his sense of touch was confused. Michael moved slowly and deliberately, penetrating deeper each time he moved toward her. Their breathing began to change as they both achieved climax. Their moaning was audible but restricted. Tess began to shed tears of joy and anguish. He looked deep into her teary eyes as her breathing returned to normal. He could see her gratification and contentment. He gently wiped the tears from her face. She stared at Michael with a look that exposed her very soul. He smiled and said, "I'm not through with you yet!" Tess's eyes widened with astonishment; then she smiled. Michael kissed her gently; the sweat from her upper lip was absorbed by his mustache. Their bodies moved together, Michael realizing that he could love again, Tess finding love for the first time, and both understanding that the situation meant they might never be together again.

Everything that comes together must eventually come apart; Michael had learned this all too well, and very soon so would Tess. Michael watched her sleep. He wanted to memorize every detail of her, sure that he would never be this close to her again. She had been that untouchable beauty he was sure he would never know. They had shared with each other, giving freely not only with their bodies but with their hearts.

He wrote her a letter without signing it. He needed to remain dead for as long as it would take to destroy the enemy or until they destroyed him. In the letter was a way for them to communicate, something she and he had shared that would leave no doubt as to who the caller was. He sat at the side of the bed and watched her for a long time. Sometime in the night, he left her there sleeping. Goodbye would have been way too hard for both of them, and he was heading for another battlefield, and it was going to get ugly.

Chapter Eight: South of the Border

The flight from Dallas to Mexico City gave Michael some time to reflect on what had become of his life and the people he loved. He doubted if he would ever see Tess again, and that meant regret he was just learning to appreciate. Josh must have received word about his death and must be mourning the loss of the father he was just getting to know. Michael needed him to be in the dark. It would be safer that way. He had called the hospital in California to see that Brittany was doing a little better and hoped that he was right about her and Josh. His eyes burned when Elle's memory made it to the surface. He was glad that she wasn't around to see what he had become again. He had not made peace with God, but found himself talking with God about his decisions. Michael knew God understood about war, whether declared by the government or not, and this was rendering to Caesar what was Caesar's. If it saved innocents from death, it was a sacrifice worth making. It was a long flight, and it gave him some time to put things in perspective. He knew he would need that if he was to be completely effective.

Edmundo Moreno was an elderly gentleman in his late sixties. He still had a full head of hair, gray in color, which made him look very distinguished. He had retired from the CIA at the request of his handlers. They had determined that Edmundo was developing some memory problems and beginning to mix up his tour guide duties with those of a government secret agent.

Michael and Edmundo had spent day and night with each other, especially after the rebellion, as they worked toward easing tension between the government and the students. They made friends very quickly and have remained in contact through the years. Michael understood the reason he was let go, and hated getting his old friend involved in his mess, but he needed two things in Mexico City, and those were a safe house and guns. He knew better than to try to bring any with him, so he stashed them in a locker at the Dallas airport for a later time.

As the plane circled the extremely overpopulated city below, he could see why so many fled to escape the poverty and corruption of the Mexican government. Even still high in the air, he could see what looked like every square inch of land occupied by Mexican nationals. He also knew that the enemy he hunted was there and that they would be protected, at least partially, by easily bought local hoodlums, who would kill their own mother for easy money. It might take some time to get the lay of the land, but as far as anyone knew, he was just another tourist visiting Mexico City, and having a private tour guide might prove to be just the edge he needed to take down his adversary.

He disembarked the plane to find his old friend waiting in the terminal. Edmundo was wearing a gray tweed suit with very wide lapels that was so old the threads of the suit were coming through the shoulder stitching. Michael threw his arms around his old Mexican friend, and they walked together with Mike speaking a form of Spanish that was almost unrecognizable as a language. Michael told him about Elizabeth's death. Edmundo gave him condolences.

As they drove through the banking district downtown, Edmundo began describing the history of Mexico City, detailing specific locations for their historical relevance. Michael didn't bother to stop him. The old man knew Mexico like the back of his hand, and that might prove invaluable in a very short amount of time. Michael leaned back and listened to the tour, smiling at the fact that he wasn't the only one getting old.

They soon arrived at Edmundo's place, which was an apartment above a bakery in the downtown area. Michael stopped in to the store and picked up some Mexican sweet bread, and then followed his host upstairs. He was given another tour of each room, and then Edmundo suggested he get some sleep. His host knew that the kind of surveillance Michael would be doing and that was going to happen after dark. Michael lay down on his bed and quickly drifted off to a long-overdue sleep.

He awoke to the sound of footsteps coming near. The room was very dark, and his eyes caught Edmundo approaching. He was carrying a weapon in his hand. Michael sat up quickly in bed.

"Buenos tarde mi amigo." The old man said smiling.

"What time is it?" Michael asked.

"It's 11:30 P.M.," Edmundo chirped back.

"Have any espresso, old friend?" Michael said, rubbing his eyes.

"Already made. Get up." The old soldier replied as he turned and walked into the living room.

Michael ran his hands over his head as he followed his friend. He raised his eyebrows as he entered the living room, because there on the coffee table was an arsenal of weapons. Michael reached out and grabbed a L.A.W. *Light Anti-Armor Weapon* from the table.

It had been a long time since he had used a L. A. W., but he remembered how to use one. It was when he was used as a point man in an allied assault. Michael knew that the enemy was expecting them, so he had moved to a location behind the Viet Cong. He was manned with six disposable rocket launchers. His diversion tactic was ready, and he let rip one rocket. Michael flashed back to a deadlier time. Then he picked up his gas-powered Stoner 63 machine gun and fired a volley at the enemy. It was equipped with one hundred and fifty rounds, so he paced his attack. He went from the rocket launcher to the machine gun until he had exhausted his ammunition. It was just what his comrades needed to overtake the hill with very few casualties.

"Here's your coffee. Drink it while it's hot." Edmundo grumbled, bringing Michael quickly back to the present.

"Am I expecting an army out there, Ed?" Michael smirked at his friend. His host wasn't laughing.

"It has become a war zone in the streets of Mexico City, my friend. The drug cartels have recruited so many men that the Federalizes cannot seem to stop them. The other problem is that many of the police are being bought off. It is a terrible situation. No one knows who to trust, so we have come to learn to trust no one. Now hurry and finish, we must take the tour of the city that I don't give to the regular sightseers." Edmundo said and handed his old comrade a revolver with four loaded clips. Michael gave him a questioning look.

"It's just in case we have trouble, it's a dangerous city, especially at night," Edmundo said. Michael smiled when he looked down and saw it was a Ruger 380.

The two men traveled by car with Edmundo giving Michael a lay of the land. They took Circuito Interior, which is a circular highway that goes all the way around the main part of the city. Occasionally, he would catch himself giving a sightseeing tour. "I can't seem to stop, amigo. I'm sorry." Michael patted his friend's shoulder. "I'll take a tour with you anytime. Don't you worry about it." Michael said as he pulled a small piece of paper from his pocket.

"My information gives this address: Paseo De La Reforma 500. Let's cruise by there, old friend." Michael said as he put the address back in his pants.

They approached the Four Seasons and pulled up to the valet parking at the entrance. Both men got out and walked inside. They made their way across a beautiful lobby into an adjoining bar where music was playing loudly. Michael was approached almost immediately by a beautiful Mexican waitress in a very short black skirt with sheer black nylons.

"May I get you a drink, senior?" She purred.

"Please two Tecates por favor." He pointed to a table in the middle of the room. The waitress nodded approval. Edmundo was already picking up intel when he found Michael and sat down beside him. He took a long drink of the beer.

"They have taken a suite on the eighth floor, but it is said that many Mexican men have taken rooms on the sixth and seventh floors as well. They are being very well paid by these men from the Middle East. They speak of an attack in Galveston, Texas. These men are concerned that there is a problem within their organization."

"You got all that before I ordered the first drink?" Michael asked with a smile.

"Bored soldiers bought for their time usually drink too much and talk even more." He smiled back. "They don't like their employers very much, but the money is very good."

Michael wanted to eliminate his targets right away, but was aware that his intelligence on their activities was very limited, and there was the problem of a friend somewhere among the monsters. He needed that person to fill in the blanks so he could find out what else they were getting ready to do to America, and then finalize his attack on the enemies of his country. If he moved too quickly, he might make a victim of the only help on the inside. When the Machine began killing, not much would remain. He needed eyes near their core to get a handle on who might be the plant.

The waitress arrived with their drinks, and Michael tipped her very well. She smiled at him. He whispered into her ear. She whispered back, and as she moved away, her lips brushed his cheek. The moment was caught by the bartender. When she got back to the bar, he began to yell at her. Michael watched to see if she could be trusted. She told the bartender that the American was very rich, then gave him the tip.

"He said this was for you and to make sure he and his friend were not made to wait for their drinks. I told the gringo I would make sure."

The bartender looked over at Michael, who had been watching carefully. Michael smiled and raised his beer in toast to his drink provider. The bartender smiled back at Michael and called him a "Puto" under his breath, angry that anyone was better off than he was. When she came back to their table, she introduced herself as Mirabelle Ortega.

Mirabelle found herself attracted to the older American. His weathered skin was the only indication of his age; his body gave him the appearance of being much younger. Michael hated that he had to lie. He had made a vow long ago to be honorable above all else, but this was a different time and a different place, and the here and now required a different set of rules. He gave her a quick glimpse of an FBI badge and told the waitress that he had been sent down to investigate the businessmen who occupied the eighth floor of her hotel. She told him that she knew that they had hired many bad men and that the women who had been hired to service them had many horrible stories about most of them. Michael picked up on most of the parts and asked if he could meet a few of the girls. Mirabelle waved at the bartender to pour two more drinks for the men. Once she brought the drinks to the table, she whispered that she could meet him in the morning at a restaurant right across the street from the hotel. They finished the drinks and gave her a hundred-dollar bill. Michael then went over and gave another one to the bartender. The second Ben Franklin began to soften the bartender's heart, and he waved graciously as the men left.

The following morning, the two men were at the restaurant waiting when a different-looking Mirabelle entered. She wore almost no make-up, pulled her jet black hair into a ponytail, and wore a tight-fitting pair of blue jeans and a white peasant blouse with multi-colored embroidery near her neckline. She was a natural beauty, and Michael noticed. She kissed him on both sides of his face and then repeated the greeting to Edmundo. She began speaking the moment she sat next to them.

"Two of my girlfriends who are prostitutes were victimized by the men from another country. Miren was beaten severely for not doing what they demanded from her. She was still recovering at her mother's home nearby. Paloma was in the hospital after being thrown down a flight of stairs. They told me the men were very perverted." Mirabelle explained to the American and his partner.

Michael asked if they could visit the women. Mirabelle nodded, and the three went out to Edmundo's car. Within fifteen minutes, they were at the home of Miren. Michael was asked to show his badge, which he did. The young girl kept asking Mirabelle if it was safe. Mirabelle assured her she would be safe.

Michael's questions were short and brief. He directed them to Mirabelle for her to translate.

"Did she remember any names?" He asked.

Miren nodded with an affirmative.

"Was there a leader?"

"The leader was very mean to the men under him. His name was Zafeer." Miren sobbed as his name passed her lips. Mirabelle translated to Michael.

"Were any of the men nice to them? If so, did he have a name she remembered?" Michael knew that this person would most likely be the mole.

"The only kind one was Khalil." She answered.

Miren began to detail to Mirabelle in Spanish the horrors she had to endure that night, her voice very quiet so that only Mirabelle might hear. She spoke of sodomy and being gang raped.

Michael's Spanish wasn't that good, but watching the face of Mirabelle as tears filled her eyes made a detailed description unnecessary. Edmundo became emotional as well, and that set Michael off.

His face began to get hard. Edmundo knew just a little bit of Michael's history from when his CIA superiors had provided information to him before they began working together in the seventies. He looked at his friend and began to see what they had said about him: "a killing machine without emotion of any kind." It meant there would soon be death in its most horrible form, and the Machine would be the cause of it.

After the three left the young woman, Mirabelle said she would take them to see Paloma. She looked over at the handsome American as they walked back to the car. She spoke softly in Spanish to Edmundo.

"His demeanor has changed. What happened?"

Edmundo told her to "La recompensa está viniendo pronto."

He then repeated it in English. "Retribution is coming soon."

When they arrived at the hospital, they were told the young girl had died from internal bleeding that morning. Mirabelle began to cry. Edmundo held her in his arms, watching the face of his friend become very different. Retribution was coming sooner than even Edmundo imagined, and it would be like nothing any of these civilians had ever seen before.

Michael and Edmundo went back to the apartment without too many words. Michael asked for his keys and made his way to the Basilica of Guadalupe. The church was filled with visitors from all over the world who had come to view the amazing cloth.

The story is told of a peasant man by the name of Juan Diego, who was traveling to Mexico City from his village, and came upon a vision of a teenage girl surrounded by light. The year was 1531, and it was December 9th, which was the feast of the Immaculate Conception. The Lady asked that a church be built in her honor. Juan went to his bishop, who demanded a miracle. Juan went back to the Lady to tell her what the priest had required. She instructed him to go up the nearby hill and pick flowers to give to the bishop. It was the dead of winter, and the flowers were not in bloom, but when he went to the top of the hill, he found many beautiful flowers all in bloom. The Lady assisted him in arranging them in his cloak. When he presented them to the bishop, the flowers fell to the floor at the priest's feet, and on the cloak was the image of the Lady.

Michael made his way to view the artifact, bowed his head, and then said quietly, "I'm going to be killing many men here in your city. If your Son doesn't want any innocents killed in the process, tell him to send them away. Things will be happening fast. He knows how I work." Michael then made the sign of the cross and turned to go. As he walked from the church, he told the Blessed Virgin one last thing. "Tell Elizabeth I might be seeing her soon."

He drove through the Mexican city, concerned that there might be someone worth saving in his next war zone. If their CIA operative was in fact with the enemy, then Michael had to somehow avoid killing him, and that might jeopardize his own safety. He needed to be completely sure.

Chapter Nine: Something Wrong

Tess rubbed her eyes repeatedly before entering Chet's office with a verbal report of the happenings in Galveston. The tears she had shed were real, but not for the reason she would be giving her superior. She could trust no one with the information she possessed about Michael, and with his letter, it became painfully clear that she would probably never see him again. She knocked and then entered.

Chet was surprised to see Tess's reddened eyes. "What's wrong, Tess?" He said with great concern.

"It's Michael, sir; I just can't believe he's dead." She began to cry.

"Michael was a good man, but he got himself too emotionally involved, and I don't think his head was right since he buried his wife." Chet declared and then continued.

"It was a car bombing, wasn't it? He apparently got too close to the terrorists, and they took him out and a number of their own as well. It looks like there was a rogue among them."

Tess added more composure as she spoke. "From the carnage, we found it appeared that the cell in Galveston was not willing to carry out the directives of their leaders. I'll put down all the details in my report, sir."

"Good, I'll need that ASAP. Michael's carelessness only cost us time in getting some answers." Chet said as he shook his head slightly.

Tess bit her lip, wanting to unload on the son of a bitch, but instead agreed and excused herself. She stood by the door for a moment and heard Chet pick up the phone and dial. She couldn't put her finger on it, but something was not right. His voice quieted when he spoke, but Tess was sure she heard the name Aqeel. It was unfamiliar to her, but it might be of some importance to Michael.

She went back to her desk and spent the rest of the day finalizing her report for Chet. She knocked on his door, but there was no answer, so she went in to drop off her paperwork. There on the desk was a notepad. She looked around, then quickly rubbed a pencil lightly over the blank pad. She tore it off the pad and quickly left the room.

Tess arrived back at her home and took out Michael's letter and then the note she had removed. On it was the name Aqeel and then a phone number. She called information to find out which country was related to the prefix number 455. It was the Philippines. Tess and Michael had been getting reports before 9/11 about safe havens for Al Qaeda in the southern area of the island of Cebu. Intelligence reports indicated that there were bomb making materials found in a raid by the Philippines' Army.

Michael's letter was full of information that he knew would only make sense to someone who knew him very well. He told her to contact him on his private number, which only Tess knew was a beeper. If she had intelligence that might aid his mission, she should beep him, and he would make contact with her. The number was the day General William Tecumseh Sherman died. She dialed 717-214-1891 and listened to a message for a waste disposal company. Her response after the beep was, "Oh, sorry, wrong number."

While she waited for his call back, she read the rest of his letter. He was very dogmatic in his desire for her to forget him. It read:

Tess, tomorrow for me is just another day to die. I'm not the young soldier who ran through the jungles of Southeast Asia. I'm slower than hell, and I am bound to get killed. If I were in a position to have a life with you, nothing would make me happier. The truth of the matter is that I am currently considered dead, but the authorities are going to pull my fingerprints before too long, and then I will be hunted by the good guys and the bad guys. Not too attractive now, am I? God and I haven't been on the best of terms lately. I know he has a plan for all of us, but I didn't like him taking Elizabeth, and he knows I'm still pretty pissed about it. Besides her, you are the only woman I have ever been with in my life. That puts you in a very select group of women I've loved. I'm headed into unknown territory now, and my only ambition is to stop these fanatics from hurting any more innocent American civilians. So pray for me because until God and I make peace with one another, there won't be anyone on my side but you. I'm saying goodbye this way because it's the best for both of us.

Suddenly, the phone rang, and she picked up after one ring. It was him.

"What have you got for me?" He questioned without emotion.

"It's a name and a number. Aqeel 455 5553785376 it's from the Philippines." She answered him, hoping he would say something to give her hope, any response that might express his feelings for her in some way…any way.

"I'll fill in the blanks." The cold voice said, then the phone went dead.

Tess wiped the tears from her eyes, not knowing if she would ever talk to him again. She took off her clothes and went into the shower. She thought about his touch as she ran the soapy sponge across her stomach. She had never been told *I love you* in so many ways without the words being said. His fingers were descriptive sentences, the way he moved them on her face and lips, and traced her laugh lines. It was as if he were a blind man trying to imagine a face by touch; once memorized, he moved on to another area, with equal attention. No one had ever loved her so completely, body, soul, and mind. She turned the hot water on a bit more and rinsed off with the removable shower head. She then stepped out of the shower and put on her lush white terry cloth robe to keep the warmth in. She went in, lay on her bed, but somehow didn't feel alone. She thought about the man who had become a killer, who was now on a mission that would lead to his death. Tears rolled down her face until she finally fell asleep.

When Tess went into work the next day, she felt something was wrong. Had someone seen her leave Chet's office the night before? Were the staff she passed in the hallway aware that she was passing information? Chet called her into his office. He immediately began to discuss a new joint effort between the CIA and the FBI.

"After 9/11, we have come to realize that sharing information is essential in defeating terrorism."

Chet continued. "For that reason," he leaned over toward her with a menacing look, "we are promoting you to liaison between the two government departments. Congratulations!" With that, Chet's door opened, and her staffers came in with a large sheet cake, singing her praises. Tess looked shocked, mostly due to her actions the day before. As it began to sink in what her duties would be, she thought that this position would give her additional access to information that could help Michael. The room was filled with merriment, but Tess couldn't help but think of where Michael was and if he was still alive.

Michael knew his next decision could be his last, but in order to avoid friendly fire, it was something he had to risk. His surveillance of the team of terrorists had been brief, but he knew after Galveston, time would not be his friend. He had gotten enough of a description of Khalil to be able to spot him on the street, and that is just where he found him.

Khalil had just made a withdrawal for the Mexican forces' payday, so he was being very careful, escorted by two of his soldiers. Michael followed them back to the hotel. Once there, he began to plan his attack and went from floor to floor. He counted two floors below the suites that had Mexican hoodlums occupying rooms. He did reconnaissance for almost an hour before Khalil appeared in the hallway. Michael made sure he arrived at the elevator at the same time. The terrorist looked at Michael for only a moment as they entered. Once the elevator started moving, Michael said very softly, "If you are one of the good guys, do not be in the hotel tonight." The elevator opened, and Michael left quickly, not waiting for an answer. Khalil was flustered by the muted message. Once outside the hotel, he found a pay phone and made a call to his CIA contact.

"What's going on?" He asked, confused.

The voice on the other end answered with a question. "Why are you calling me?"

The terrorist plant described his brief encounter.

"He's not one of ours." The voice said.

"Then I may be compromised," Khalil suggested.

"Get the fuck out of there!" The voice said emphatically.

"Not possible! I still don't have all the details of the California mission. If a dirty bomb makes it into the U.S. and is detonated, the destruction will be catastrophic." Khalil sighed, frustrated over his situation.

"I'm sending in the Calvary. They will be in position by…" There was a pause as the voice looked at his watch. "It's almost seven your time, expect a visit by midnight."

"Okay, I'll try and get Zafeer to give me details. Try and find out about the wild card, could he be one of the maniacs that slaughtered the cell in Galveston?" Khalil questioned getting more distressed.

"If it is one of them, we are totally in the dark. They sound like some Special Forces group, but they haven't made any contact with authorities or us, but they must have some awesome intelligence to find you. So just be careful." The voice cut off abruptly.

Zafeer was sitting on the couch when Khalil got back to the suite. He greeted his boss and went to the bar to pour himself a drink. Zafeer watched his second in command drop two ice cubes into the glass and then pour some Johnny Walker Black. He turned as he took a drink.

Zafeer said, "That looks good. Pour me one for my brother."

Khalil began to repeat the process as Zafeer came over. As he handed his boss the glass of good scotch. He could sense that something was very wrong. Zafeer took the glass with one hand and then grabbed the neck of Khalil and began to lift him off the ground.

"Anyone else I could believe, but you, I can't believe you would turn on me." Zafeer couldn't finish his sentence; instead, he took the glass and broke it on Khalil's head, knocking him unconscious.

It was almost ten o'clock in the evening when the undercover agent's eyes focused on the wall clock. Zafeer's eyes twitched with anger, seeing the now-tied Khalil begin to come to. He struck him again, bringing on another reprieve from the beating. When he came to again, it was almost ten thirty. He knew that his cover had been blown and that after a long torture, he would be killed just as he had seen his insane commander do so many times in the past two years.

"We must talk, old friend." Zafeer had gotten drunk waiting for Khalil to reach consciousness. He looked down at the traitor and began to reveal how he found him out.

"You know that I don't trust anyone. I had you followed for the past three months. You had been seen making phone calls from public telephone booths when you always carry a cell phone. Why, I asked myself, would he need to do that? My doubts about you were confirmed today. I had you follow. Who were you speaking with on the phone before you came back tonight? What did you tell him? Are you the reason my Galveston plan was ruined? I want to know who you work for before I kill you...But I am not going to kill you too quickly. I want to hurt you very much first, just as you have hurt me with your deceit. I trusted you like a brother, and you have betrayed me."

Zafeer pressed the button on a small stiletto knife and then plunged it down into the flesh just above Khalil's right knee. It quivered as Khalil screamed into the room. Zafeer struck his face with his fist and then turned away, joyous over the pain he was causing this traitor. Suddenly, he heard noises down the hallway outside his suite. Something was wrong, very wrong.

Chapter Ten: Salvation

The warm, humid night was reminiscent of Viet Nam in the spring. Michael's Machine mode was in full operation, and he wasn't planning on taking any prisoners. Edmundo had supplied him with enough of an arsenal to handle twice the enemy forces that were in play. Michael's adrenaline was flowing, and that needed to be curtailed if he had any chance of succeeding, and success would be measured by the element of surprise. The Mexican forces needed to be removed first as quietly as possible. He looked down at his watch. It was ten twenty-five. He stood near the service elevator in black clothing. On his utility belt were five smoke bombs, two grenades, a survival knife with an eight-inch blade, two three eighty pistols with silencers attached, and four clips each holding twelve rounds. In his hand was his personal killing weapon. His count was six on the sixth floor in two rooms, nine on the seventh floor in three rooms, and one Mexican at the door of the suite. Inside the suite were hopefully only eight terrorists if he had been right about Khalil.

He moved against the wall near the first room. The door opened as a very drunk Mexican yelled back in Spanish that he was going to get another woman for them to play with. Michael reached down and opened his killing ring. The door closed. Michael appeared in front of him and shoved the blade deep into the man's throat in the proximity of his vocal cords. There was only a muffled gurgling as he went down. Michael then tapped at the door. If his count was right, there would be one at the door and only one more inside to deal with. The voice inside could be heard cursing, "Did you forget your key, Puto?" When the door opened, Michael's revolver sent a barely audible bullet into the man's heart. He held the man as a shield momentarily until he found the third man sitting on the couch with a woman's head between his legs, his pants down by his ankles. He tried to get to his weapon, but the silencer put a large hole in his head before the woman could free her mouth from its task. She instinctively began to scream, but Michael held her mouth and, in Spanish, asked if there were any more soldiers in the room. She shook her head negatively. He whispered for her to get her clothes and leave quietly. She got up, grabbed her clothes, and headed out in the hallway, stumbling into her pants while trying to cover her breasts. Michael heard the door open to the next room of hired soldiers and a voice making its way to where he was standing. "Why are you chasing the pretty whores away...?" He never got a name out, as Michael put a hole in his nose. His body hit the floor with a loud thump, and suddenly, he could hear two or more men preparing for a battle. Michael pulled a smoke grenade and let it fall near the door of the adjacent room. He went inside through the smoke, his ring blade making contact twice in a matter of seconds with arteries, and two more of the soldiers bled to death on the floor.

Michael bolted up the stairs to the seventh floor and dropped another smoke grenade in the stairway before he closed the door. He knocked on the door of the three connecting rooms. "There is a fire." He said in his best Spanish. The men moved quickly through the doors as Michael sat on the floor picking them off as they moved through the hallway, ensuring that he had a visual on each target, sure that there would be some women in the mix. His count was eight more soldiers down. He stood crouched down as he made his way through the smoke-filled doorway of the last room. He saw the flash of a revolver and replied with two silenced blasts and waited as the thud of the body found the carpeted floor. The screams of a woman filled the air, which meant to him that he was almost out of time.

Michael looked at the elevator door and decided that this might be a nice approach since it opened near the door of the suite. He stood on the side expecting gunfire into the lift and wasn't disappointed. His revolver put an end to the noise of gunfire as the gun-riddled guard fell toward him.

Michael pulled the pin of a grenade and knocked on the door of the suite. Suddenly, automatic fire splintered the wood of the door as bullets fired through. Michael waited until it came to a stop, then kicked the damaged door open and dropped in the grenade. He could hear men scattering until the explosion sent debris and body parts back through the doorway. He carefully made his way inside, counting dead bodies as he went. By his count, there should be only two terrorists left, not counting Zafeer. He felt a stinging in his left arm as the sound of gunfire rang through the air. He was grazed by a bullet. Michael looked up towards Heaven and said, "Is this how you're getting rid of me?" Another bullet rang out, identifying the enemy's position behind a luxurious red velvet sofa. Michael placed his weapon on the floor, pointing at the sofa, and fired six rounds. The terrorist jumped up in pain and was met with a fast traveling survival knife into the chest. All of a sudden, the room was quiet. Michael carefully made his way into the next room, where he found Khalil tied to a chair, his head down, and a knife sticking out of his right leg. A quick pulse check meant he had arrived just in time. Michael quickly made his way through the rooms to be sure he was no longer in danger. Zafeer and one of his soldiers had escaped through the back entrance of the suite.

Michael went back to claim his knife and then used it to cut the unconscious man free. He hadn't planned on bringing anyone out with him, and in just a few minutes, the place would be filled with the Mexican police. He examined the leg, wrapped it with a torn piece of cloth from the bed sheets, and then pulled the stiletto from his leg. Michael pressed the button, which closed the blade, and placed it into his pocket. He put the man over his shoulder and made his way out the back of the suite, down the staircase, and out the door, all the while watching for any enemy who might wish to risk their life against his force of unknown size. Edmundo was waiting in the back lot behind the wheel of his car. He saw Michael carrying a body. He quickly drove to Michael's location, swung open the door, and questioned, "You been shopping?" Michael only smiled, gently placed his guest in the back seat with Michael slipping in beside him. He tore the pant leg to get a closer look at the wound. The knife had penetrated the rectus femoris muscle but just missed the femoral artery. Michael was relieved. They moved out of the back parking area as police sirens and black sedans entered the complex. Michael watched through the back window to ensure they were not observed.

"You need to get in touch with the CIA," Michael said softly to his friend as they drove through the city. "Drop me off at your place, and then take him to the hospital. Tell the agents to meet you there."

"What do I tell them?" Edmundo asked.

"Tell them I told you to come over," Khalil said weakly. He turned to Michael and asked, "Who the hell are you?"

"Forget you saw me, that's the charge for saving your ass," Michael said as the two men stared at each other.

"Okay, but do you have a name?" Khalil asked sincerely.

"You can call me Mike." His liberator said.

The CIA agent put out his hand, "Thanks, Mike."

"You're welcome," Michael said.

"I could use any info you could help me with. Word around is this Zafeer is planning something big in the States. Do I have it right?" Michael asked.

"Zafeer is insane, he is planning an attack at the Governor's conference in Los Angeles, and his men are already in motion," Khalil answered him weakly.

"Anything else?" He inquired.

"Yes, it is a suicide mission." He said, wincing in pain.

The car pulled next to the curb, and Michael jumped out, disappearing into the darkness.

A few moments later, the soldier found his way to the bathroom of Edmundo's apartment and pulled off his black shirt, exposing the skin wound on his left arm. He began speaking to the God he had been enraged with. "Okay, yes, I need you if I'm going to make a difference in this holy war." He started to bandage his wound with alcohol and a four-by-four from Edmundo's medicine cabinet. "One day, we will have to have the conversation, and you know what conversation I'm talking about. For now, let's just agree to get along." He fell back on his bed, took a deep breath, and stared up at the ceiling. "Thanks for keeping me alive today." He closed his eyes, and sleep came quickly.

Chapter Eleven: Regrouping

The Mexico City luxury hotel was filled with police and cameras flashing from local news stations. The reports found their way into the offices of the Pentagon in the United States. Tess was glued to the television, looking intently for an image of the man she loved. She knew who caused the massacre; her only thought was whether he survived the engagement. She listened to the TV reporter as she gave a description of the incident.

"The latest report we have is that a Mexican drug cartel has made a vicious assault against some international businessmen who were staying in the penthouse suite. The information is sketchy at best, Tom, but we will try to update you when the Mexican police are through with their investigation. Tammy Roberts for ABC News in Mexico City."

Tess bit her fingernails nervously, hoping to hear about Michael, and praying she wouldn't. She began making calls to the CIA for information from their department heads, but they were completely in the dark, except that they received a call that a retired agent had saved their mole.

It was late in the morning when Edmundo arrived back at his apartment. Michael was fixing himself a cup of coffee.

"Want some?" He asked in a morning voice.

"I need sleep...I have been interrogated all night." Edmundo said wearily. "Okay, I'll have a cup."

"Should I be worried yet?" Michael queried.

"No, my friend, with the damage you did, they never suspected that only one person was capable of such carnage. How is your arm?" Edmundo asked as he walked over to him to inspect the wound.

"It's just a scratch, but you'll need to replenish the first aid kit," Michael said with a small smile.

Edmundo's face got serious. "The package I dropped off at the hospital had a lot to tell me before the Feds showed up. Something bad is going to happen in L.A. Khalil said that a W-54 backpack nuclear weapon was already in your country, he thinks San Bernardino, and they wanted to create hell on the west coast of California." He looked at his friend but got no response. "This war you're in will end badly for you, my friend."

Michael sipped his coffee and just made an affirmative noise in response. Edmundo reached out and squeezed Michael's good arm, sat down with a cup of espresso. He gulped it down all at once, immediately got up, and headed for the bedroom.

"I must sleep now."

Michael didn't respond; he just poured the rest of the small pot into his cup and walked onto the balcony of the apartment and sat watching the new day begin. In a few hours, Edmundo would be under investigation, and it would no longer be safe for him. He looked around the streets below, then opted to finish his coffee inside.

The Pentagon was buzzing with activity as agents from the CIA and FBI met in the large, newly repaired conference room. Tess and

Chet Avery were discussing the bloodbath in Mexico City with some military brass in attendance. An old General spoke quietly.

"This has the look of a military attack. Do the Mexicans have a counter-terrorist group capable of this?"

"Not that we're aware of, General," Tess spoke up.

"Well, whoever did this was able to assassinate over twenty men in a matter of ten minutes or less and then disappear with no witnesses. Oh, that's right, except for the CIA operative who had been discovered and apparently rescued by an old ex-CIA agent who just happened to know the mole, got his address from an anonymous source, and just happened to be there after the shooting stopped. Oh yeah, let's not forget that the ex-agent must be close to seventy with Alzheimer's disease." The General said with obvious irony.

The representative from the CIA, David DeBolt, looked around as all eyes seemed to be focusing on him.

"Our department was not involved in this operation; however, the end result saved our agent. Khalil had penetrated a rogue cell that was being led by a madman. Zafeer El-Amin had every intention of blowing up the refinery in Galveston Bay and had decided to make an attempt at killing our President. Khalil is being debriefed as we speak, and hopefully, we will have a better understanding of what happened down there." DeBolt said.

"Zafeer, unfortunately, is still loose, and we need to know if he had any other plans of destruction," Chet said as a matter of fact and then continued. "Let's adjourn for now and meet after the CIA has been briefed by Khalil Nadiman."

The room began to clear. Chet grabbed Tess by the arm and quietly asked her to wait. She rustled with the papers on the conference table until they were alone.

"I'm not sure what happened in Mexico, but it's beginning to sound like the group involved in the Galveston carnage might have gone south," Chet said as he looked deep into her eyes for some kind of response.

Tess could tell he was fishing to see if she might have information she had been withholding. She looked back at him without blinking and asked him, "Did you send a special ops unit to Galveston, Chet?"

His head moved backwards slightly. "Of course not, Tess."

Her question made him feel comfortable that she didn't know anything, so he decided to share his concerns.

"I'm beginning to believe that the CIA, CENTCOM, or DOD has had some involvement in these two attacks. They have decided not to share it with the FBI...typical bureaucratic bull shit!"

Tess responded. "I agree, Chet. I'll find out what I can."

"Just keep your eyes and ears open, Tess," Chet said.

She left the room feeling better that Michael was still off the radar, but she was unsure how long that would last. There was a message on her answering machine from her agents in Southern California. Tess called back and reached O'Connor.

"What's up, Kyle?" She asked.

"We have Brittany going through hypnosis, and she has been able to remember a lot of what she saw in the briefcase of Doctor Rashad a day before she was shot. Here's the thing, Tess, she said there were notes that indicated that an Al Qaeda cell in California was going to bring in a small nuclear device and set it off in downtown Los Angeles. I don't know how accurate the information is, but it's supposed to take place at the National Governors' Association, which is in August." Kyle explained. Tess asked suspiciously, "All this from a glance at papers that fell out of a briefcase?"

"The hypnotherapist said that under the right circumstances, the mind acts like a camera. She also saw two names that were underlined, Muhammad Faqih and Hakim Faqih. What do you want us to do?" Kyle asked for directions.

"I'll report this to Chet, and we'll get our agents to provide extra security, but if they get a bomb of that magnitude into the city, it won't matter where we position anyone, they'll all be lost," Tess said pragmatically.

"What about Brittany?" Kyle questioned.

"Get her set up with a new identity, and have her get registered into a nursing school program in Orange County," Tess answered.

"Got a name in mind?" Kyle asked sincerely.

Tess thought a moment and then said, "Call her Sandi Thomas."

"Where'd you get that name?" He asked with a smirk in his voice.

"It's my parents' names," Tess responded. "It will be easy for me to remember."

Tess went to her computer, accessed the CIA database, which she now had access to, and pulled up the Faqih names. The information about them gave goosebumps on her arms. They were a sadistic pair who had been working in Pakistan on their nuclear program. The two were suspected of torturing one of the Pakistani scientists until he was dead for information regarding a W-54 nuclear device. The following day, the body of the scientist was found, and the brothers were gone. They had mutilated his body methodically, according to the government forensic report. These men were dangerous, but Tess didn't pick up any information that would put the two in the suicide bomber category. They would probably hire a few zealots for that honor.

Agent Jeremy Worley of the CIA wanted to know what happened to his undercover agent, but wasn't getting any answers that could help him understand. Khalil Nadiman repeated over and over again, "I don't know how many men were involved in my rescue, but I am thankful."

Jeremy began to interrogate, "Did they talk with you?"

"No!" came the response.

"What were they wearing?"

"Black. They were all in black with utility belts."

"You're a trained agent, you're taught to memorize everything around you in a crisis situation, and you can't remember anything about the men that saved your ass," Worley yelled out of frustration. "How do you know the old man?"

"I had a fucking knife in my leg and was knocked out at least twice. I can't remember everything. I met the old man when our group took a city tour right after we arrived here." Khalil yelled back.

Worley left the room and met with the rest of his team, located down the hall, watching the interview. They were discussing the possible forces involved in the extraction of their man when Jeremy walked in.

"What do you think?" He asked the men in the room.

Tim Tinella, his second in command, spoke first. "We need to get a tail on the old man ASAP. He's old, but I think he's the way to go on this. I don't know how much I'd remember after the beating he got."

Jeremy turned to Michael Crider. "Stake out the old man's residence and see where it takes you."

"Yes, sir," Crider said with respect and exited the room.

Michael had spent the morning packing up his gear and preparing for a flight to Los Angeles through Dallas, Texas. He needed to stop what could be worse than 9/11, and he didn't know how much time he might have. He had altered his look again, this time shaving off the goatee completely. He wore a red baseball hat that read "Mexico" embroidered in white, and a pair of sunglasses. When he picked up his bag to leave, Edmundo walked in from his bedroom.

"Were you not going to say goodbye, compadre?"

"Thought it might be easier that way. The less you know, the less they will bother you, and you know they will be bothering you." Michael assured his old friend.

The men embraced, and Edmundo said, "I will pray for you every day, amigo."

"Thanks, my friend, I'll need it." Michael headed out the door.

A taxi was waiting downstairs, and Michael got into it. Across the street, agent Michael Crider got a very bad photo of the unknown American leaving. He wondered if he should follow the taxi, but thought better of it and remained on watch at the apartment. He called Agent Worley to let him know about the unknown person. Worley wondered who it could be, then instructed Crider to bring the old man in again for some more questioning.

Michael arrived at the Benito Juarez International Airport, which was crowded with travelers from all over the world, and left the cab wearing a black baseball cap with the New York Yankee insignia. Security was incredibly deficient compared to the extra precautions that were being taken in the United States. He was glad since his only objective was to get out as soon as possible. He knew that he would be heading into Southern California fairly blind, and there might not be time to do any surveillance. His cell phone began to ring after touchdown at Dallas/Fort Worth. He looked down, sure already that it was Tess.

"Hi, beautiful." He said cheerfully into the phone.

"I'm glad you're alive." She told him with a sigh.

"Me too!" He said back to her.

"You made quite a mess in Mexico City. Where are you now?" She asked.

"Deep in the heart of you knows where." He answered with cryptic humor.

"I don't have much to tell you except they are planning a nuclear attack in Los Angeles." She told him solemnly.

"I got that already. Was hoping for more details." He said quickly.

"I've got two names, Muhammad and Hakim Faqih. These are two sadistic brothers who have the skills to pull this attack off. I'm sending agents to cover the Governor's Conference in downtown Los Angeles, so you'd better stay low, but Michael, if you can't stop this, stay the hell out of the L.A. area. These two brothers are bad news, but I'm thinking they have a suicide squad for the detonation." Remember, sweetheart, you're not twenty anymore." She said in almost a wifely way.

"Yes, dear, but my info says things are being set up in San Bernardino. So keep your troops away, because if the bomb goes off, it will be there." Michael warned her lovingly.

"I want to see you again," Tess confessed.

"The intel doesn't make it look promising." He said almost jokingly, then added, "But it would be nice for me too. If I save the west coast and survive maybe we could make a date."

"Oh, you always have something to do, don't you?" She teased him back.

"Let's just play it by ear. Fair enough?" He queried more seriously.

She came back with, "Fair enough!"

Chapter Twelve: A Purveyor

Michael had settled in for the flight to Ontario, California, and closed his eyes to rest. His mind quickly careened through the past few weeks and the multitude of dead bodies. He thought about General Sherman. Michael began to realize that the day the Muslim terrorists struck the towers in New York, war had been declared against America, a war that transcended borders, but more importantly, a war that included civilians as potential targets of attack. For him, it was justification for his violent actions. They had declared a war without rules of engagement. Michael had plenty of experience with that kind of war. He had been trained in it. So Michael was going to bring the hellishness of war to them, and he knew how to make it personal and ugly. This war would not have R & R, or would it have an ETS date, except for the one God had planned for us all. So this was a war to the death, and based on the intelligence he had, it could be really soon.

The announcement to prepare for landing brought him out of his thoughts. He straightened his seat as the plane moved through the sky over the 10 freeway. He looked out the window at miles of industrial buildings as the plane made its way onto the runway.

Ontario had grown into a suburb of greater Los Angeles, and the airport took some of the congestion away from LAX. Michael couldn't help but think about his son Josh. He wondered if he and Brittany had made a connection. He was thinking too much. He needed to focus. Michael rented a car under his alias, Mark Santana, and headed for San Bernardino. The freeway was very congested as he traveled eastward. He wondered why air travel always seemed to land around the time everyone was getting off work and going home.

Michael had two names and very little time, so he checked himself into a Super Eight on Hospitality Lane, went into his room, pulled out the yellow pages from under the night table, and went to hotels. He knew that these men would choose a top-of-the-line hotel, so he started by calling the Hilton.

He called and asked to speak with Muhammad or Hakim Faqih.

"I'm sorry, we have no one by that name registered here." The voice on the line said politely. Next, he called La Quinta Inn. He asked to speak to Muhammad Faqih.

The voice on the line said. "Yes, sir, I'll ring him."

A moment later, the voice said. "I'll connect you."

The room phone rang three times with no answer. Michael hung up. The hotel was within walking distance of his motel. He got into his car and drove over with his bag. He asked if he could get a room. The desk clerk said he had a room available, number 317. Michael told the clerk he'd take it. He headed up to the room. Always the strategist, Michael planned how he might attack his enemy if this was the location fate dictated. He needed some weaponry, and downtown San Bernardino was a great place to get guns. He took some large bills from the lining of his bag and headed downtown.

He considered his enemy and assumed that if they were soon planning to die, they would want to partake of the pleasures of man. Animals like Atta and his crew all acted alike. Michael was getting into a killing zone as he recalled the horrendous slaughter of

September eleventh. He noticed a gentlemen's club right on Hospitality Lane. He would be going there as soon as he got armed.

Michael pulled into a tattoo shop on E Street with a sign that read Bingo Baba Bing original art done here. He had known many artists who hated losing business due to a lack of funds, who would take anything of value as payment for a great tattoo. So he recognized an opportunity to secure some weapons without any documentation or waiting period. The artist inside was a friendly guy. He had full sleeves and even a small parrot tattooed on his face. The room was filled with tattoo art on display, and Michael looked at each wall carefully, then turned toward the artist.

"I'm looking at your work, it's quite impressive." Michael reached out to shake his hand.

"Call me Bingo." The artist shook the hand of the stranger, then asked, "What can I do for you...?" He was waiting for a name.

"Just call me Matthew. I'm in need of a few weapons that I understand you might have in your possession." Michael lied to Bingo.

"Oh, I don't carry any weapons. I'm an artist." He said cautiously.

"Listen, Bingo, I'm not the law. I just came in from out of town, and I'm after some real bad guys. You know I can't lie to you about being a cop." Michael said with sincerity.

"What exactly are you looking for?" Bada Bing asked as he looked Michael over carefully.

"Something easy to hide under a coat and maybe something in an automatic design." He said, wanting to be as vague as possible.

Bingo got up, walked over to the door, and locked it. He told Michael to have a seat. He went into the back room and came out a few minutes later. He was holding a revolver in his right hand and carrying a black plastic case in the other.

"You're not a cop, right?" Bingo said, still holding the revolver.

"I can assure you I am not the police," Michael said, looking right into Bingo's eyes.

Bingo flipped the gun handle forward so Michael could inspect it. Michael took the gun and looked it over carefully. It was a Smith & Wesson 629 revolver, single and double action, 44 Magnum, with a 6.5-inch barrel. It had a finish of stainless steel, 6-round capacity, with a red front sight and an adjustable white outline rear sight. He had used the same weapon when he was a field agent with the bureau, where he won first-place medals for seven consecutive years for distance accuracy at one hundred yards. He turned the weapon to see that the serial number had been filed off.

"This will be fine. What else do you have?" Michael questioned.

"You'll probably like this." Bada Bing said, opening the case.

Inside the case was a 9 millimeter Uzi with a silencer attachment. Michael picked it up and began to measure its weight and balance. It had been a long time since he had one in his hands. Bingo carefully watched his customer and finally asked.

"Have you used one of these before?"

"I've had some practice in the past." Michael declared.

"Are you interested?" Bingo asked.

"I'll take both. How much?" Michael asked without taking his eyes off the weapon in his hands.

"I'm thinking about a thousand bucks?" Bingo was highballing him.

"No problem. I'd be interested in anything else you can come across." Michael said, still fingering the automatic weapon.

"Sure," Bingo said, excited that he had gotten the price he wanted.

He continued, "I'll be honest with you, I hated having this in the store. If the cops ever saw it, I'd be looking at a felony." Bingo got up, went into the back again, and came back out with a box of ammo for the revolver and a bag with three full clips for the Uzi.

"These are on the house. I overcharged you." Bingo confessed.

"Great, you saved me a trip. You're a good man, Bingo." Michael said gratefully as he reached into his pocket and pulled out a wad of hundreds and dropped it on the counter. Bingo picked it up and counted out ten. There were four hundred left. He handed them back to Michael.

"Consider this a tip." Michael smiled.

"I'll use it to get my daughter the computer she wanted, thanks, Matthew," Bingo said.

Bingo unlocked the door and let Michael out. He watched as the stranger got into a late-model sedan and disappeared around the corner. He went over to his phone and dialed. "You know that computer you wanted? Well, Christmas looks like it's coming early, sweetheart. No, I'm not kidding. I'm closing the shop for the rest of the day to take you to the store." Bingo hung up, turned over the open sign to closed, and locked up. He smiled, thinking to himself, "I like that guy."

Chapter Thirteen: Conflagration

The soldier entered the Flesh Club and remained just inside the door to allow his eyes to adjust to the darkened room. The rotating red lights accented the room, giving off a seedy, sensual feeling. He made his way around the stage where a half-naked young girl danced seductively, removing her sequin bra, then began swinging around a pole. She stopped suddenly and winked at the new stranger, hoping it might mean a lap dance later. Michael heard the name Muhammad. He was being called by his brother, who was getting great pleasure from being dry rubbed by an experienced girl who moved her hips like an appliance.

Michael sat a few feet from them near the rear of the room so he could get a sense of how many were in their party. He sat for almost twenty minutes watching until his count was complete. He was approached by three or four beautiful young girls who rubbed his bald head and pleaded to let them pleasure him. His comment, "just watching for now," sent each away until a beautiful woman came from behind a curtain and made her way towards him. He began to react. She looked like Elizabeth, and all he wanted to do was get her out of the horrible place. Michael was losing his concentration.

The woman could see that she was getting a response from him. So she didn't say anything but just sat next to him. Michael tried to keep his mind on his targets, but her perfume penetrated his senses.

"My name is Kim, what's yours?" She whispered into his ear.

"You need to move along, sweetheart," Michael said cruelly.

The girl moved even closer, her breath making contact with his ears. "Wouldn't you like a good time? You're looking very stressed."

Michael turned towards her with a look of death coming soon. She became frightened and was quick to get up when the announcer called her name as the next act. She couldn't understand his behavior, but got up on the stage as the loud seductive music made her automatically gyrate around the stage. Her attention turned to the stage hounds ready to dispense singles for a closer look.

Michael got up. He had made his assessment of the situation. There were ten men in the Faqih party, and he would eliminate all of them if he could. Two men got up to go to the bathroom. It was his cue to begin. He followed them inside. He slowly opened his ring weapon. While they urinated, he stabbed one man in the spine, who fell back with a moan. The other man turned toward Michael, and the blade swept through all his neck vessels and sprayed the tiled wall with bright red blood. He came out and moved through the dark. He passed two men on his right and sent the weapon deep into the axillary artery just behind the clavicle bone of each man. Blood shot into the air as each man's heart beat just a few more times before they collapsed. Michael knew this would then set off the alarms. His revolver roared as a bullet made contact with one of the men, who noticed what had just happened. He was given a third eye as the back of his head exploded onto the dancer who was gyrating on another bad guy. Her scream fell silent after seeing her patron's head detonate from the next projectile. She passed out and fell back to the floor. Another dancer threw herself to the floor, giving Michael a clear shot at his next victim's chest, dropping him into forever. Hakim got a shot off, but Michael saw it coming and dropped to the floor, answering back with a bullet that caught the terrorist on the left side of his face, leaving most of it on the stage. The next victim he caught running away in terror, only to be stopped when the .44

magnum blew his chest out. Muhammad had jumped up on the stage and grabbed Kim, who was standing there in horror. Michael needed him alive to find the weapon of mass destruction. Suddenly, Kim's stomach burst slightly as a bullet from Muhammad's revolver attempted to kill this unknown assailant. His aim was poor, but watching Kim fall set Michael off, his weapon fired directly into the right arm of his enemy and sent him back against the stage curtains and then to the ground. He made his way to Kim. It was clean through and through. He applied direct pressure and told the announcer, who was huddled behind the bar, to call 911. One of the girls, who was still shaking on the ground nearby, responded immediately when Michael told her to come and hold pressure. He walked over to Muhammad, who was bleeding profusely from his wound and praying in his homeland's language. Michael ripped the long-sleeved shirt from his shoulder and then tied the sleeve around his upper arm to stop the blood flow.

"Time to go, big boy." Michael declared as he pressed his finger into the arm wound, causing Muhammad to scream like a little girl.

The lone soldier guided him to the door, then turned and said, "These were bad men who wanted to hurt our country; the less the authorities know about me, the more of them I'll be able to kill." Michael and his prisoner disappeared out the door.

Fire trucks and an ambulance arrived on the scene within a few minutes, and so did four police cars. Their job was to keep the crime scene as pristine as possible, and that is just what they did. Kim was alert and oriented when one of the police officers came to her and asked what she saw.

She said loudly, "All I know is there was gunfire, then someone grabbed me and shot me in the stomach."

165

She was told that a detective would be by to see her when she was feeling better. The girls all followed her to the ambulance.

She looked at all of them and said. "If he were just killing people, we would all be dead. He knew every person he was after, and no one else got hurt." The paramedics placed her in the ambulance, and she was taken to the county hospital.

Police detective Gil Astric arrived on the scene. He was a seasoned officer and had gone through the gang wars of the Inland Empire during the late eighties. Upon entering the building, he felt as if he had entered a warzone. He walked around the stage area and went from one body to another. He kept muttering under his breath, "Son of a bitch!" A policeman had gone into the bathroom to relieve himself and came out white in color.

"Sir, there are two more in the men's room."

Astric muttered, "Son of a bitch!"

He went inside the restroom. He first saw the blood splatter on the yellow tiled walls. He looked down to see a gaping hole in one man's neck. The other man didn't look like he had been hurt, so Astric put his fingers on the man's neck and got a pulse.

"Call the paramedics back. This guy is alive. Son of a bitch!"

Chapter Fourteen: Dissection

Michael was counting on Tess's intuition that Muhammad wasn't keen on being a suicide victim himself. He had brought the terrorist to the Super Eight motel using the side entrance after his attack at the Flesh Club. Once inside, he tied the fanatic to a chair and inserted a terrycloth towel into his mouth. Michael didn't have a lot of time to get the information, so he would be delivering an extremely large amount of pain in a very short time. Michael at first thought of removing his digits as he had done to Bijan, but realized that it would leave a hell of a mess for housekeeping to clean up. Instead, he took the enemy into the bathroom, still tied to the upright desk chair, and laid the chair in the tub so that Muhammad was lying supine. Michael moved his face under the faucet and turned the water on fast. He counted to ten, then shut it off. Muhammad was gasping for breath. Michael was silent and turned the water on again. He counted to fifteen, shut the water, and quickly removed the wash rag from the terrorist's mouth. At first, the man did nothing, then suddenly, a cough and a large amount of water was expelled from his lungs.

"Who? What? Where? When?" Michael said softly to the man still gasping for breath. Before he could answer, the water again was turned on full force over his face for the count of ten. Again, he asked, "Who?" before he got to what Muhammad yelled out, "Two of my soldiers, they are carrying the bomb, to kill your Governors." He coughed a few times, then blurted out, "Tomorrow at the Convention Center." Michael wanted more details. He began the process again. Michael was impressed with how much the fanatic could tolerate. After about four hours, the counts got shorter, and the extremist began to spell out all the details of the operation. The leader had even given him the license plate number. Michael had all the information he needed to stop the act of terror, but would he be able to prevent them from carrying out their mission? He calmly put the wash rag back into Muhammad's mouth and turned on the water. There would be no reprieve this time. He put on some gloves, wiped down the room of any fingerprints, got all his gear, and eventually went back into the bathroom one last time. He shut the water, staring at the dead, open-eyed Jihadist who would never gasp for air again.

Once he got behind the wheel of his rental, he contacted the police station and asked to speak to the detective in charge of the Flesh Club incident.

"This is Detective Astric. What can I do for you?"

"I left you something at the Super Eight on Hospitality Lane, room 208. Check the bathroom." Michael said softly.

"Who is this?" Astric asked, his voice rising.

"I'm one of the good guys," Michael said and hung up.

Astric was still holding the disconnected phone, "Son of a bitch!"

When Astric arrived at the Super Eight motel room 208, he brought a forensic team in to look for fingerprints or anything that might help him discover the identity of the killer. His cell phone went off just as he discovered the body in the tub.

"Hello." He yelled into the phone.

The voice on the other end informed him that the man found in the bathroom of the club had regained consciousness. Astric looked down at the body, still wet from the torture. He thought to himself that whatever the hell was going on was not the act of a crazy man. His fear that it could be some kind of terrorist activity prompted him to call the FBI.

Astric had made it to the hospital bed of John Doe, who was stabbed in the back, only minutes after FBI agent Kyle O'Connor had arrived. The officers introduced themselves, and Kyle tried asking questions of the wounded man. He had been given pain medication intravenously, and it didn't appear that the agent was going to get answers right away, which gave the two men time to talk.

Detective Astric proceeded to describe the scene at the Flesh Club, which piqued the interest of O'Connor.

"What you're describing, Gil, is very similar to what went down in Galveston, Texas, and Mexico City, but there were no witnesses at either of those locations. What are the eyewitnesses saying?"

"Here's the thing, O'Connor, we couldn't get any of them to provide corroborating information. Some said there were three men, others two. No one gave the same hair color or height, or weight. Hell, it's as if they were trying to make it impossible for us to get a handle on the group." Astric admitted with frustration.

O'Connor excused himself and went outside to make a call. He tried to reach Tess Lamia, but she wasn't in her office. He then asked to speak to Mr. Avery. Avery answered the phone and listened as his West Coast agent told him about what he had learned. Avery contacted Tess on her cell and relayed the information, "Have we gotten any fingerprints from the crime scenes in Galveston or Mexico yet?"

"Not yet, but we should have them soon enough." She replied, biting her lip as she drove through the city. Tess knew that it would only be hours before Michael's prints showed up in either Galveston or Mexico.

"I'll call you as soon as I hear something, Chet." She assured him and hung up.

Tess couldn't do anything regarding what was about to happen, which meant that Michael would no longer be listed as dead but as alive and wanted by the FBI, CIA, and law enforcement agencies in two countries. She sat in her car looking out through the window in thought until the car behind her honked, forcing her to move again through downtown Washington, DC.

The traffic of Los Angeles was as thick as mud; occasionally, cars would switch lanes and move another few feet. Michael got off the freeway and took a frontage road to make better time. He was informed by the late Muhammad Faqih that his zealots were driving a 1994 white Ford Econoline van with white paint covering the logo that had been printed on the sides. They were told to arrive at the convention center by two o'clock while the Governors were in session. Michael looked at his watch. It was just after nine thirty in the morning. Michael hadn't gotten any sleep interrogating the enemy soldier, and the congested trek was only making his fatigue harder to control. His head bobbed occasionally as sleep tried to overtake him. His fear that he alone might not be able to stop the terrorists prompted him to contact Tess.

"I'm in LA traffic, and here's what I have for you. Two men in a white 1994 Ford van with license plate number 65133H are heading for the convention center. Get the information to the men on the street and pray either they or I get to them before they get to all of us." Michael tried to be cheerful.

"You sound tired, Mike." She said, concerned, and then asked.

"Are your fingerprints going to be found at one of the crime scenes?"

"Probably, I really didn't think I'd get this far," Michael answered her, and suddenly noticed the van in the right lane of the freeway. "Got to go." He said, and the phone went dead. He needed to get back on the freeway. He noticed an on-ramp just ahead and pulled out the 44 magnum. He got on just behind the van and verified the license plate. The traffic began to get bogged down again, and the lane stopped. Michael got out of his rental with the cannon at his side. He tapped at the Van window. It slowly went down, and Michael asked the driver, "Did you bump me?" At the same time, he counted heads. Muhammad had spoken the truth to just two men.

The 44 magnum came up and blew the head off the driver. Brains and blood soaked the passenger, who had little time to react as his chest exploded an instant later. Michael went to the back of the van and pulled out the backpack. He placed it on the back seat of the rental, got back in behind the wheel, and drove off the freeway, leaving the van blocking commuter traffic.

Chapter Fifteen: Exposed

The Pentagon FBI chief was confused, as the latest information from Mexico City was that deceased agent Michael Angelino's fingerprints were all over the crime scene. Chet Avery wanted to tell Tess himself because of her close relationship with Angelino. She saw Chet, a file in his hand, standing near her office as she walked through the C corridor with a cup of Coffee in her hand.

"What's up, Chet?" She asked as she approached him.

"Let's talk inside your office." He responded in a very serious tone.

Tess acted surprised when he dropped the file onto her desk and told her that Michael was alive and might have been responsible for all the killing that had been happening over the past few days. She put her hand over her face. Chet gave her a moment and then continued. "Michael wasn't acting right since 9/11, and then his wife died. I'm afraid he must have cracked. I had his records pulled up, and I discovered his early military record. Tess, I think Michael is responsible for all this shit."

"I can't believe that, sir." Tess lied.

"He was a fucking assassin for the government, Tess, a trained killer." Chet tried to convince her.

"Chet, he's in his fifties. He's been behind a desk for over twenty years." She said, trying to cause doubt.

"Well then, he must be working with someone. O'Connor reported that the eyewitnesses in California said there was more than one assailant who attacked the men in the club." Chet replied, attempting to reason the mess out. The office phone rang, and Tess picked it up. She said yes twice, then hung up.

"The threat to the Governor's conference has been eliminated." She told Chet.

"How?" He asked.

"Apparently, a car stopped on the freeway, a man got out, killed the two terrorists, then pulled something out of the van, got back in his car, and drove off the freeway." She said, describing the report she had just received.

"Michael?" He questioned.

A moment later, her cell phone rang. She nervously looked down and saw that it was Michael. She turned to Chet and said, "It's my mother, excuse me for a minute." She stepped outside her office and immediately asked, "Had a busy morning?"

"Yes, I have." He answered, then continued. "I have a delivery for your West Coast agents. Tell them to have the Los Angeles bomb squad go to their parking lot, where they will find a 2001 Ford Taurus. In the trunk is the W-54, it looks like a military backpack. Oh yeah, tell them to be careful."

Tess waited until he was finished, then said, "By the way, they are on to you. They think you have help."

"That would be you, darling." Michael joked, feeling better since the threat of a nuclear disaster had been stopped.

Chet opened the door impatiently.

"I'll call you later, Mom. Bye." Tess said lyrically.

"The voice on the other end replied. "Bye, sweetheart."

"Sorry, Chet." She apologized as she went back in, sat down, and opened the file.

"I can't believe Michael could be capable of all this." She said emotionally. She added, "He told me he was having blackouts that were lasting for days, and I told him to get to the doctor for tests. The last thing he told me was that he would do just that because it was freaking him out. What if he isn't even aware that he's doing these things?"

"We can't have a mentally unstable vigilante on the streets killing people!" Chet said in a rage. "Some of the victims may be innocent bystanders, for all we know. Our people are working with the CIA on this." He declared as he made his way to her office door.

"Tess, contact all FBI offices and give them a picture of Michael. We need everyone inside the Bureau looking for him. Tell them to proceed with caution; he is only a person of interest at this time, but we need to get him in here." Chet ordered.

Once the door closed, Tess took a deep breath, happy over the fact that Chet wanted to cover up anything that had an ex-FBI agent crazy and on the loose attached to it. She contacted her agents on the West Coast and told them to go to the Los Angeles Police Department. She indicated that she received an anonymous call that they would find the bomb in the trunk of a Ford Taurus. She gave them all the details they needed. After she hung up, Tess made another call, this time to the airport for information about flights leaving for L.A. After that, she pulled a picture from Michael's file. It was the last one taken while still with the Bureau. The image showed a gray-haired man with a full beard, slightly overweight, and Tess thought to herself, "This one will be just right." She smiled to herself.

When the news of two terrorists killed on the freeway in Los Angeles reached Zafeer El-Amin, he had just arrived at the Badian Island Resort and Spa at Cebu City in the Philippines. The international news was being broadcast on the large flat screen television in the lobby. His plan had been thwarted by unknown forces, which savagely destroyed his Mexico City operation. His temper remained under control as he called Saudi Arabia.

"I am in the Philippines and need brave men who are willing to die for Allah."

"Whatever you need will be provided to you, Zafeer, but explain to us how your soldiers were overtaken by two or three men in black costumes." The voice on the other end waited for an answer.

"They must be mercenaries of some kind." He said with less authority.

"Failure is not acceptable, Zafeer. Be warned that our tolerance of you will be short-lived if you cannot bring about the terror to America that you promised." The voice became stern.

"Our Al Qaeda cells here will assist me in delivering devastation to the port of San Francisco, but I need my brothers from home to ensure that the operation is successful." Zafeer requested humbly.

"We will transfer funds to you at the Far East Bank in Cebu. The men you requested will be on a plane today and will arrive the day after tomorrow. There will be twenty of our best. I want the details before you begin the undertaking. That is all." The voice on the phone disconnected.

The voice on the line was Sheik Zahiem, a powerful financier who worked in the office of King Abdullah. He turned to Nami Sirhan, his right-hand man. "You will go to the Philippines. If Zafeer is unsuccessful again, kill him."

"Yes, Sheik," Nami answered and then immediately left the room.

Chapter Sixteen: Wanted

The female student was gawking at her television when the picture of her hero flashed across the screen. "Michael Angelino, who was originally thought to have been killed in Galveston, is now wanted by the FBI as a person of interest who might have information about the massacre that took place there." Sandi Thomas was still wearing bandages under her clothes from the gunshot wounds she received just days before the massacre they described. She picked up the phone and dialed Joshua Angelino. He was at his drawing table when his phone rang, and he answered in his professional voice. "SPJ Architecture, may I help you?"

"It's me…" She hesitated, still not used to her new name, "Sandi."

"Hi, I was just thinking about you as I was drawing," Josh replied while he smiled.

"You had better sit down because this will be hard to take." Sandi took a deep breath and spit out the news. "Your father is alive!"

Josh was silent. Sandi continued. "He is wanted for questioning about what happened in Galveston."

Joshua's mind was racing over the reports he had read about the horrible killing spree in Texas. He had hoped that the reports about his father were wrong. He heard his name called through the phone line and answered with a question. "Were there any specifics?"

"No, just that he is a person of interest. My God, Josh, they had his picture on the television like he was a criminal or something." She explained emotionally.

"I'll call his old office to see if they can give me more information. They must know something. I'll fill you in over dinner, okay?" He asked, already knowing the answer.

"Okay, I'll see you later," Sandi replied and hung up the phone.

Joshua was pretty sure that his father was responsible for the killings, but wanted someone to verify it. He knew Tess and his Dad had been close, so he called his father's old number. He was redirected to a switchboard and then transferred to Tess's office. Tess picked up after the first ring. "Hello, Agent Lamia."

"Tess, it's Joshua Angelino." He said.

"You heard about your father?" She asked.

"Yes, but are they sure he's alive?" He wanted someone to tell him what he prayed was true.

"Yes, Josh, your father was continuing to have blackouts. He went AWOL, and his fingerprints were found at both crime scenes. He needs to come in so we can get this situation under control. Your Dad was investigating a terrorist cell in Galveston, and we believe he killed them all brutally." Tess explained.

"You said Terrorists, the same ones that attacked us already? They deserve to die. Did he hurt any innocent bystanders?" Josh asked proudly, but was concerned that his father's blackouts might have loosened some screws in his head.

"As far as we know, they appear to all be a part of a plot, but there are some people we are still unsure of their association with the Al-Qaeda cells, and for that reason, we need him to come in." She explained and then added, "If he should call you, please plead with him to give himself up to the FBI." She needed him to be aware of the situation as it was being handled.

"Thanks, Tess, if you get any information about him, please let me know, and if he contacts me, I'll call you right away." Josh hung up the phone and said a prayer. "Dear God, don't let my Dad kill any innocent people."

Michael was sitting in a brand new Chevy Malibu, which he rented under the name Mark Devlin. He was watching the planes coming in over the smog layer that made L.A. so famous, waiting patiently for Tess to arrive. He had time to think about what he had done, and he found himself in a conversation with God.

"Thanks for keeping me safe, Lord. I know you are in charge, and if there is a way for all this to end, please make it so, if not, please forgive me in advance for what I am likely to do."

Michael thought about calling his son. What would he tell him? He wondered how he could justify to his son the actions he took.

He looked down at the throwaway cell phone and dialed Josh.

He spoke softly. "It's me, Josh."

"Are you okay, Pop?" His son inquired sincerely.

"I picked up a few scratches. My body is beat to hell. I've been using muscles I haven't used in a very long time, son."

"I called Tess; she wants you to give yourself up." He said, then continued with emphasis on his next question. "If you think you are doing the right thing to keep us safe, do you stop? I've been praying for God to give me an understanding of what you are doing, and I'm pretty convinced that this is a war, regardless of what the politicians want to call it. Dad, you do what you think is right, and if I can help in any way, just call me. I'm so proud of you, Dad, no matter what they might say about you."

Michael had not felt tears fall since Elle passed, but to hear his son say those words was something he never thought he would ever hear. He thanked him and then said, "I'd better go. I'll call again." He looked out the window as the sun was going down. It was a beautiful sunset, the kind that makes you sure that God must be an artist to create such beauty. Suddenly walking out of the terminal was another example of God's genius. She stood just outside the baggage claim area, looking around as the cars moved past her. Michael smiled and drove out of the airport parking lot, pulled up, and pressed the window to go down.

"Need a lift?" Michael asked seductively.

"Sure." She responded and threw her bag in the back seat. She got in and kissed his lips. She took a second look.

"What's different about you?" Michael had shaved his moustache off, leaving just a black goatee. She ran her fingers across his upper lip; then kissed him again. She kept her hand on his face and looked deep into his eyes.

"You've been busy, are you alright?" She asked with true concern.

"I got nicked in Mexico, but nothing too serious. Have you gotten any information about Zafeer?" Michael was still in battle mode.

"Our CIA operative has indicated that Zafeer has been spotted at an exclusive hotel in Cebu City, Philippines. Are you going after him?" Tess inquired.

"Khalil told me the animal is hell bent on killing as many Americans as he can. It's retribution for the death of his mother. I'm catching a flight out tomorrow morning at eight. This one needs to be stopped forever." Michael said, knowing she understood.

"That doesn't give us much time, then." She remarked.

"Just a few hours, but hey, I promised you a date." He smiled at her, and she melted into his arms.

They drove to a small motel on Fourth Street. Michael went to the counter. A small Chinese man stood behind the reception desk.

"May I help you?" The tiny man asked.

"Yes, I'm working at the hospital, and I need a place to crash for a few hours." Michael lied.

"How you pay?" The bell clerk asked with a very thick accent.

"Cash," Michael responded.

"Your name?" The small man inquired.

"David Rogue," Michael answered and placed three twenties on the counter.

"Okay, Mr. Rogue. You be in room 217. Have nice sleep." The clerk passed him the key.

Tess met him by the elevator, and the two went to the room. There would be no sleeping over the next few hours as two bodies became one. Michael remembered everything that excited her and ensured that it happened. Tess held nothing back as she gave herself completely to him. She kissed him around the wound, trying to make it all better. Michael appreciated the effort. His hands traveled over her whole body. He wanted to touch every part of her. After a few hours, they lay next to one another with his feet near her head and her feet near his head. Michael examined her freckles, wanting to remember each one of them. She giggled as he moved from one to another, kissing them after a careful examination. They were new lovers and couldn't get enough of each other. His kisses found their way to her upper thigh, and she responsively opened herself up to him. They sweat themselves into a passionate frenzy, their bodies moving to a natural rhythm. The conversation of their bodies stopped with exhaustion, and the verbal conversation started with Tess.

"I love you so much it hurts right here." She said, pointing to her heart. Michael wanted to lighten the mood because, before too long, he would be out of her life again.

"It hurts on your breasts?" He raised the question, staring at her beautiful, naked breasts. Tess grabbed a pillow and hit him over the head with it. Michael grabbed a pillow to retaliate. They laughed as the pillows made contact. Michael pretended to be really hurt, causing Tess to come to his aid, which allowed him to get one last pop to the body, making her fall onto the motel bed.

"You're a cheater." She said with a silly laugh.

"Sometimes that's how you win." He remarked, raising one eyebrow.

Both could sense that time was running out. They spoke of what was to come, with Tess wanting instructions on how to reach him overseas. He assured her that he was going back to his old stomping grounds and that he would make contact as soon as he touched down. She wanted to tell him to be careful and that he wasn't a spring chicken anymore, but she kept it to herself. He had just outperformed anyone she had ever been with, so she just bit her lip.

"They're looking for you everywhere, Mike. The picture I gave them was the last one you took in DC. I'm pretty sure that with over twenty pounds gone and your white Santa beard reduced to a black goatee, you shouldn't have a problem for now, but if, for some reason, you get stopped...God, Mike, don't try to run." She said, thinking of a potentially horrible end to his life.

"Tess, you can't worry about me. If God wants me gone, I'll be gone. It's really that simple. Do you want me worrying about you when I'm in the middle of a war?"

"Of course not." She interjected.

"It only takes one slip-up to be dead, so I don't have that luxury. Do I love you? Yes, of course I do. Would I like to go home and retire with you by my side? You bet, but how could we be happy if people we love are getting blown up? These Jihadists want to destroy America. Civilians are now a part of the battle, and you well know they don't play by any rules of war. Tess, I've waged war against this kind of enemy. I was trained not to pay attention to the Geneva Convention but to get the job done. I'm going to bring the gates of hell right to their door, where they are plotting to hurt us. They're not going to know or understand what is happening to them, and they will die horrible deaths at my hands. I will bring fear to their wretched lives like they have never known before, and the leaders will wish they had never been born." Michael said firmly and then kissed her hard on the lips.

"I love you, Michael." She sobbed as she got the words out.

"Don't love me too much, Tess, just in case."

Chapter Seventeen: Philippines

Michael watched as a beautiful Asian stewardess approached him, smiling. He had already settled in for the fourteen-hour flight, hoping to catch up on some much-needed sleep. The beauty asked if he would like a pillow and a blanket. Michael nodded and thanked her. His body wanted to sleep, but his mind raced over the past few weeks.

"Lord, I've had this conversation with you one other time in my life. I need you to watch over me and protect me as I enter into this war with Muslim extremists. I will vanquish those who try to hurt the innocent. I will constantly remind them that if they plan on waging this war, I will make it painful and I will make it ugly. I still expect you to explain why you took my Elizabeth from me, but that can wait until we see each other face-to-face. In the meantime, watch over Josh and Brittany and especially Tess. I know it was probably wrong to get involved with her at this time in my life, but you didn't make me perfect, and I'm just a man. I know that's a copout, but I'm tired and can hardly think. I love you, Lord, so forgive me of all my sins, and I understand I'm here at your discretion. Amen." Michael closed his eyes and fell into a deep sleep.

The Machine had prayed that he would never be resurrected, but fate sent him on a course destined for his own ultimate destruction. Michael concluded that the enemy was brewing a major hit on the port of San Francisco, and it was being spearheaded by Zafeer El Amin in the Philippines. His intelligence was limited at best, and with no help in an area of the world he hadn't seen in close to thirty some years. The other big question was who was Aqeel and what did he have to do with all this? The Machine was only thirteen hours away from what might become his last battlefield and some unfinished business with the enemy. The only good news was that there would be no enemy on the plane, and that meant uninterrupted sleep.

The next thing he felt was a mild tap on his shoulder. His eyes opened to the smile of the Asian beauty, and he quickly readjusted his seat for the landing. He was beginning the preparation deep within his inner self for battle. Michael would need weapons when he arrived in country, which shouldn't be too difficult in Cebu City, which had a reputation for loose women and murder for hire.

From his internet research, Michael knew where to go and how to act, so he wasted no time once he went through customs. He stepped into a cab near the airport entrance and asked to go to APL Trading on Salinas Drive in Cebu City. Once they arrived, he asked the cab to wait for him, dropping a twenty over the front seat.

The guy behind the counter watched closely as Michael walked slowly up to the counter after viewing the rows of ammunition down each aisle. He waited until the clerk spoke in very good English.

"What can I do for you, mister?"

"I need a 380, a 44 Magnum, and a long-range rifle with a high-power scope," Michael said as a matter of fact. The salesman smiled at Michael.

"What you doing? Going to war or something?" He questioned jokingly.

"Something like that," Michael replied.

Michael picked up four boxes of ammo for the rifle and eight boxes for each revolver and placed them all on the counter. The attendant stopped smiling as his customer's face suddenly got hard. The soldier from America put down five hundred-dollar bills.

"Give me change in pesos," Michael said, watching the man pull out his calculator. Once the transaction was complete, he took his new tools, got back into the waiting cab, and was instructed to go to the Pulchra Resort near Mango Avenue, which was an area noted for loose women and getting information for a price.

The lobby to the resort was exquisite with light brown marble floors and counters. The hotel manager came over after seeing Michael pull out a wallet stuffed with hundred-dollar bills.

"May I help you, sir?" The manager said as he pushed the hotel attendant away from the counter.

"Yes, I would like a very private suite," Michael said politely.

"Do you have a reservation, sir?"

"No, I just got in from the states, and I was told you were one of the best places in town, but if you don't have room, I'm sure the other hotels will be able to accommodate me," Michael said politely.

"No Problem, sir. What is your name?" The manager said quickly, wanting to close the deal.

Michael reached into his pocket, pulled out his passport, and opened it on the counter.

"Thank you, Mr. Doe. How long will you be staying with us, sir?" The director asked as he put in a series of numbers on his key machine and handed Michael a plastic key card.

"I'm here for some important business meetings, which should take about three days, and then I'd like to take a few days to enjoy your city. It's my first visit to your country." Michael lied to the supervisor.

"If you need anything, please contact me, no matter what time, day, or night." The manager said as he handed Michael a business card with his name on it. Michael read the card and extended his hand.

"Thanks, Ronald Albo. I will." Ronald was a bit surprised at how nice the new guest was and shook his hand with great pleasure. Ronald then turned to the bellhop and ordered him to help the new guest.

Michael's luggage was carefully placed on the clothing cart, and he was escorted to a luxurious suite. He moved around the room, taking in all the amenities. The bellman finished placing his luggage near the small closet and asked if there would be anything else. Michael smiled thoughtfully and slipped him a twenty; something he could never afford to do on his government salary, but that was a lifetime ago, and he was learning to adapt. The bellman bowed graciously and left, gently closing the door.

Michael had always wanted to take Elizabeth to exotic places, but their conflicting schedules and paying for Joshua's education left them no time and little money. Now he was traveling first class and had acquired a fortune from his enemies.

"Maybe I should have done this sooner, Elle." He said as he looked toward Heaven.

The soldier couldn't dwell on the past. He was on an assignment first for intelligence and second to kill an unknown number of bad guys. His aging body was sore all over. So he stripped down, put on a bathing suit, and headed out the screen door to the pool and Jacuzzi. After a few laps, he settled into the warm spa and placed his sore muscles in front of the powerful jets. This would be the only time he had for himself, because in a few hours, he would be heading to the seedier side of the Filipino nightlife.

He dressed casually with a white shirt and a pair of Levi 501 jeans. He slipped the 380 in his front pocket and two clips in his back pocket. He put on his personal killing device and made his way to the hotel lobby. He was met by Ronald.

"Mr. Doe, where are you going tonight, because you must be careful in the nightclubs?"

"I'm just going a few blocks from here to the Del Mar and the Lucky Lady on Mango," Michael answered.

"You must not carry too much money. Best to put the taxi fare in your shoe so you can get back here. The girls will want you to buy a drink. Many sad stories, but you no listen too much or fall into their trap. If you need a companion, I know clean girl named Alice. She is physical therapist but now doing massage because no work here for too many girls. Please be safe, okay?" Ronald remarked, looking very concerned.

"I promise I won't bring home any girls," Michael assured his host.

With that said, Michael hailed a cab near the entrance to the resort and was quickly whisked away to his first bit of reconnaissance at the Del Mar. When Michael walked into the bar, the women began to make their advances, hoping each would be picked by the American stranger.

Michael moved near the bar, and a sultry Filipino girl not much older than eighteen made contact with his arm and was awed by how very strong he was.

"I'm looking for information, doll, and if you can get me good intelligence, it will be more than you can make in a year here." He whispered into her ear.

"I'm Miranda Cortez. You buy me a drink at the private table." She said loud enough for the bartender to hear.

Michael nodded. Miranda escorted him to a more private table near the back wall. He noticed about four tables over a heavy-set man in his forties being rubbed to satisfaction through his pants. He looked deep in her eyes, held her face in his hands, and spoke very softly.

"Listen, Miranda, I'm not here for a blow job or hand job." He kissed her lips lightly, then continued. "I need information about a very bad man who is somewhere in Cebu City. I will pay very well for this information." Again, he kissed her very softly to ensure the bartender could see she was doing her job well. "Are you the girl to get me this information?"

Miranda had never been kissed so gently, and it made her shiver inside. She only nodded at first; then, after getting a grip on her emotions, she asked him.

"What is his name and what do you need to know?"

Michael told her the name of Zafeer.

Miranda's right eyebrow rose slightly.

"I have heard this name from my uncle." She said very quietly.

"I need to know how many men he has with him and where they are staying, and I need the information as quickly as possible," Michael informed her.

"I get information. What is your name and where are you staying?" She asked.

"I am John Doe, and I will be back tomorrow night at the same time. If you don't have the information by then, I will find someone else, and you will see no money, understood?" He wanted to make sure she knew he would be finding other sources.

Michael leaned over and kissed her lips very softly while holding her face with his right hand. When he pulled away, her eyes remained closed. He believed he had made an impression.

"Tomorrow, Miranda." He said, then got up and left the bar, but not before he dropped a twenty-dollar bill on the bar for the bartender.

Michael stepped outside the bar where a line of cabs had congregated. He took the first one, asking to get a brief tour of the city. As the car moved down the street, Michael looked back to see the bartender pointing at his cab, and then two young men got into the cab.

"Step on the gas and take a few side streets, I think we're being followed," Michael said, raising his voice. The cabby did as he was told. Michael watched the cab move farther away, and then he told the cab to stop at the next bar he saw. A few moments later, the cab stopped in front of the El Gecko Resto Bar. He paid the tab and stood outside until he was sure the other cab caught sight of him. He walked into what appeared to be an Irish pub. There were just a few people at the bar, a few more at one of the many tables, and a Filipino girl and a gentleman playing pool.

He made his way to a staircase, and halfway up, he heard the door of the pub open. He continued into the naughty bikini bar. It was the smallest one he had ever seen, with barely enough room for twenty customers. He made his way across the room and headed for the men's room. As he moved through the door, he adjusted his ring so that it became lethal. He waited behind it as the two young men came in, one with a blade at the ready. Suddenly, the would-be attacker looked down at his left wrist as blood squirted profusely from his severed radial artery. The other barely moved into the room when the ring found its way into his right eye. The ring made two more lunges from one neck to the other. The continued movement was limited to nerve endings that had not received word that death had arrived. He quietly walked from the bathroom and made his way downstairs and into the street. The cab he hailed was just moving away from the entrance when a woman's scream could be heard. Michael didn't bother to look back. He sat back and viewed the city by cab for about an hour as the taxi driver gave him a verbal tour of Cebu City at night.

He slipped his card in the door and waited for the green light to indicate it was open. His senses were immediately sent into alert; someone was inside, he could feel it. He quietly moved toward the bathroom, the door was ajar, and suddenly he heard a female voice humming softly. Michael pushed the door open a little. A beautiful young woman bowed to him and said hello. She was dressed in a pink sheer blouse and a pair of short shorts revealing very beautifully curved legs.

"I am Alice Fedorka.

"Hello Alice." He said, smiling at her.

She bowed again, then turned toward the sink and rotated the faucet to the hot water. It began soaking thick white terrycloth towels.

"Mr. Albo told me I should give you a massage because you just arrived from America and that you would be very tired from the journey." She explained.

"I am tired." He admitted, his eyes finally moving away from her and thinking about his latest crime.

"I am ready for you." She said as she stopped the flow of water.

"How do we do this? He asked, unsure of the local custom.

Alice handed him a medium-sized dry towel and turned away.

"Oh! Okay." He said.

He took his clothes off and loosely wrapped the towel around his waist. While he positioned himself on the massage table, he noticed her picking up his clothes and folding them neatly on a chair. He started to relax as her oiled hands moved over his neck and back. He watched her small feet from the slot on the table and wondered how such a tiny person could have so much strength. When she moved to his arms, she noticed the recovering wound he received during the attack in Mexico. She was careful not to apply too much pressure. His whole body hurt, and he knew it was because he was old, too old for what he had gotten himself into.

"Why are you here…is it vacation?" Alice asked as she began to rub more warm oil on her hands.

"There is a man known as Zafeer El Amin who has come here to try and do more harm to America, and I need to find him before he hurts many more people," Michael admitted as she relaxed him. The name caught her attention, but she continued her without speaking.

Her hands were comforting once she kneaded out the stress knots beneath his skin. He was almost unconscious when she straddled his legs and pulled the towel down, exposing his buttocks. He became very embarrassed at first, but soon forgot to be as she dug her fists into his gluteus maximus, and after removing all stress in that region, he was fast asleep, until she asked him to turn over. Sleep returned almost as fast as he turned.

When he opened his eyes, Alice was humming while she folded towels. He wiped a bit of drool from the corner of his mouth and then noticed she was in a very high-cut nightie with no panties.

"How long was I out?" He asked gently.

"Just half an hour." She answered as she continued working.

"It was wonderful. You have gifted hands." He remarked as he sat up on the massage table, noticing her long, beautiful legs.

He was taken off guard as she moved between his knees and opened the towel, exposing him completely. She smiled as she began to lower herself, her hands moving up his thighs. Michael grabbed her wrists and moved her back into a standing position. She assumed it was to kiss her, and so she moved closer to his face.

"You have the wrong idea, Alice." He stated while looking deep into her eyes.

"Mister Albo said to take very good care of you." She insisted.

"You have taken very good care of me, Alice. He assured her.

She again moved to kiss him, but he picked her up by the shoulders and placed her on the sink counter. She pulled her legs up and looked sadly at him. Michael, sensing she was feeling rejected, placed his hand under her chin and looked her straight in the eyes.

"Nothing would give me greater pleasure than to be with you, but it just isn't the right thing to do. I have someone special waiting for me back in America, and this would hurt her very much. Do you understand?"

"You are a good man, and I understand. I go now." She answered as she slid off the counter and pulled on her jeans.

Michael took two hundred-dollar bills from his wallet and slipped them into the front pocket of her jeans. He kissed her cheek. She hugged him tightly, then grabbed her folded table and left.

The world Michael now found himself in was nothing like where he had been. He kept telling himself that this was a jungle just like the ones from Viet Nam, and he could be attacked at any moment if he let himself get off guard. He fell back onto the bed and looked up to Heaven.

"I wonder how much of this is your doing? He asked God.

"You could have picked a younger guy. I'm aching all over. Is this why you took Elle…because of the mission? She wouldn't have handled it very well. She told me her prayers were answered when I got the desk job in the Pentagon. Guess you knew that already. Anyway, watch over me, Lord, cause tomorrow could be full of death."

Chapter Eighteen: All in the Timing

Nami Sirhan arrived without warning in Cebu City. It was eight-thirty in the morning. The hired henchman was used by Saudi Arabia to assassinate any enemy of King Abdullah. He was a grim-featured young man with a detailed beard that framed his face. His hair was very short and jet black in color. His eyes were dark brown, intimidating, and he was almost six feet tall with a physique that indicated he spent countless hours in the gym. The King had handpicked Nami for his position as a hired assassin and paid him very well for his services.

The king was concerned that Zafeer was becoming a liability to the cause of reducing America's presence in the Middle East. He had instructed Nami to eliminate Zafeer regardless of his success, for the loose cannon had allowed himself to be infiltrated by a CIA operative. Abdullah liked Zafeer's idea of destroying the port of San Francisco and perhaps a million Americans in the process. He was sure this would be just what was necessary to have the infidels running with their tails between their legs. He had surmised that the American people had no stomach for war. Their young people were not disciplined, and he had noticed they were not getting educated in the principles that created the United States, a perfect combination for his Muslim faith to become entrenched within their borders. Those who resisted would be killed as an example to the weak, and they would then follow like the weak sheep they had become. Regardless of the wonderful plan, Zafeer's fate had been ordained upon completion of the attack on San Francisco. When Nami arrived in Cebu City, he telephoned Zafeer, who indicated they would come by helicopter to pick him up. The twenty jihadists would be picked up by car.

Tess Lamia was never one to sit back and watch in a crisis, and to see the man she loved highly outnumbered in a foreign country was not sitting well with her. She pulled Michael's file and began researching his military career. After an hour of reading, she came across the name Xavier Sanchez. She began to look for any information she might unearth on him, which did not take her very long because Mr. Sanchez had numerous arrests on his record, mostly for drunken brawls in San Antonio, Texas, where he was currently serving a thirty-day sentence for beating up a Marine. She contacted an FBI field agent in San Antonio and told him to get Sanchez transferred into Federal custody for suspicious involvement in terrorist activity and to escort him to Washington, D.C. Tess was planning a reunion for Michael, whether he liked it or not.

Chet Avery was in one meeting after another with little time to be directly involved with the day-to-day workings of the terrorist task force. Tess was working very hard to have things in order for her new boss, Ted Hobson, and from what she had heard, he was aggressive and strictly by the book. He had spent twenty years as an officer in the Marine Corps and then took a job for the State Department; Chet had been watching Ted carefully since Michael had lost his wife as a possible replacement for the task force. Tess knew she only had a limited amount of time to provide any assistance for Michael without being exposed as an accomplice to his murderous spree. The gossip around the water cooler was that there wasn't a whole lot of effort in finding Michael and bringing him to justice for the murder of Dr. Rashad Naseem and the other businessmen in Galveston. The FBI task force was finding it very difficult to believe that a bald, elderly man, who had been at a desk for over twenty years, was even capable of such a remarkable hit.

Upon arrival at the FBI Pentagon offices, Xavier Sanchez was still rubbing his head from a severe hangover. He perked up immediately when Tess Lamia walked into the interrogation room, where he was placed, handcuffed to the table. His weathered face tried to put on a pleasant smile, but it wasn't coming off too well.

"My God, you're X. S.?" Tess said, shocked at what he looked like.

"Only one person has ever called me that, and based on the news reports, he is dead. So why have you brought me here?" Xavier responded with disdain.

Tess walked out of the room and told the agent sitting outside to take a coffee break. Once he was gone, she went back inside and sat close to her prisoner.

"Your old friend isn't dead, at least not yet, but he is in a dangerous situation and could use some help." She said quietly, then added the question. "Interested?"

Xavier's face changed suddenly, as did his demeanor.

"Where is he?" Xavier asked.

"Philippines." She answered.

"When can you get me there?" He questioned her.

"You should arrive in Cebu City by ten thirty in the morning their time. Tell me what weapons you need, and I'll get them for you, but understand this type of operation will come with no back-up. The government will deny any knowledge of the operation if you get caught." She said clearly so he understood.

"Just like the good old days," Xavier said with a half grin.

"For sure, I'll need an Accuracy International AWM rifle with a Schmidt & Bender PM II/MILITARY MK II scope, that way it won't matter where the targets are and I'll have a bit of a distance advantage, night vision gear fatigues, some fragment grenades and some disposable anti-tank missiles and anything else your guys think I might need for me and my partner. Why are you helping him?"

Tess couldn't answer like she wanted, but assured the old soldier that the FBI didn't want a rogue agent who might have had a mental breakdown to be killed in a country far away. She told him that since 9/11, he had been having blackouts.

"We want Michael back to get a medical evaluation and to find out if he got himself mixed up with mercenaries and who they might be working for, and where they got their intelligence on the Galveston cell. Mostly, I want my old boss to get some professional help."

"Lady, you are so full of shit." The old sniper wasn't buying it for a minute.

"You're in love with the Machine. I could see that in a drunken stupor." He continued.

"Fuck you, Xavier, and just get ready. You'll have everything you need, so make a detailed list." Tess was angry that her feelings were so obvious.

The shadow for the Machine smiled and gave her a small gestured salute.

Michael was still sleeping when he heard the knock on his door. He put himself on high alert, got into a pair of shorts, and placed the 380 in his hand. The peephole gave him a distorted view of Alice. She started to knock again as he opened the door.

"Good morning, Alice." He said politely.

"Morning Mr. Doe, I have some information for you." The young girl said quietly.

"Come in." He said as the door opened a bit more for her to enter.

He placed the weapon in the drawer by the door as she moved past him and sat on the bench at the foot of his bed. Michael put a short-sleeved shirt on, checked his clock, which broadcast in digital letters seven thirty in the morning, and sat beside her.

"The bad man you spoke of last night is on Badian Island. I heard his name before. My father told my brother Honesto to go and work for him because money is very good. He is paying many men to be on the island with him as security. My brother went last night to Badian Resort and Spa. My brother good boy, but my family needs money." She said as she pulled a cell phone from her purse and punched a few buttons, then turned the phone towards Michael.

"This is my brother." She said as she turned the photograph toward Michael.

Michael's photographic memory recorded the image, knowing this would make the hit more complicated. He assured Alice that everything would be alright. Alice hugged him tightly and told him Thank you and left.

Michael needed to move quickly in order to end the madman's plan. He armed himself with his array of weaponry and called to charter a helicopter. Michael began working on a plan while the taxi made its way to the Mactan-Cebu International Airport. It was just turning eight twenty.

"Element of surprise." He thought to himself. "That might be just what the doctor ordered."

It was nine in the morning in Cebu City. Miranda Cortez wailed openly upon hearing that her two friends had been killed the night before. She told the police, who were investigating the crime, that they had been following an American. A man named John Doe. Officer Palawan rolled his eyes upon hearing the name, but assured the young woman they would be checking it out. He then asked her for a detailed description, which she gave him. When he asked Miranda why the two men were following the American, she lied and said that the man had roughed her up at the Del Mar, and they had followed him to exact judgment on him.

Officer Palawan called in the description, and an all-points bulletin was established to be on the lookout for an American going by the name John Doe. The bulletin also described a bald white man with a short goatee and moustache, black or dark brown in color, approximately six feet tall. He is a person of interest in the killing of two Filipino men. The time was ten fifty-five.

It was eight fifty-five when Zafeer sent four SUVs to pick up the twenty men, and he arranged to take the helicopter to pick up Nami from the airport. It was a two-and-a-half-hour drive each way, but just thirty minutes for the copter trip to Cebu City. Zafeer was a bit anxious and didn't want Nami to wait too long for fear that it would compromise his relationship with the king. He caught the helicopter at nine. He had told his only surviving aide from Mexico to stay in the suite until his return.

"I will call you Gabir if I need you for anything. I'll be back with our guest in about an hour and a half. Contact the front desk and indicate we will need two or three more suites." Zafeer indicated to his subordinate.

"As you ask, Zafeer," Gabir responded.

Gabir was a soldier with no misconception as to his place in the hierarchy of the Zafeer organization. He was glad to have come through the Mexico City attack alive and, through attrition, found himself in a commanding position.

Tess received a distressing call from the CIA that an American was being sought for the death of two Filipino men. She could tell by the descriptions that Michael was at work, but she had not heard from him since Los Angeles. She needed to make contact with him, so she dialed the waste disposal number and left the "wrong number" message; then waited. She had already missed dinner.

Michael had just arrived at the airport when his beeper went off. He would make time to answer because he was heading into enemy territory and might not come out alive. He dialed quickly en route to the helicopter pad, where one was waiting for his arrival.

"Talk fast." He said abruptly.

"I received word from the CIA that you started working already. They have a description of you, so be aware." She instructed her hero.

"That was an unavoidable distraction from my task." He said coldly.

"I've sent you some assistance..." She began but was interrupted.

"What are you doing? You know I work alone." He barked into the phone.

"I sent an old friend of yours by the name of Xavier Sanchez, you called him X. S. He will be arriving by midday your time on a private jet. If you don't want him, send him home, but despite his looks, he seems pretty capable to be of some assistance. Your choice." She said with a sense of authority and then continued.

"Don't expect me to stand by while the whole damn world is breathing down your neck. I love you, so I can't be all that rational. Got it?"

"Got it. Did you give him my number?" He asked, less mad.

"He knows how to contact you. If you accomplish this mission you'll need to get your ass out of the Philippines. Need an exit plan?" She asked.

"I'll figure something out, but keep the phone close by just in case. It would appear we are still a team." He said affectionately.

"That you can count on." She answered.

"The war will be starting sometime today, so I'm out." He said and disconnected. It was just after nine.

Chapter Nineteen: Beginning of the End

Michael made his way to the Bell 206B helicopter, a light-weight, single-engine that held four passengers, showed his fake ID, and boarded, handing the pilot American dollars for the one-way ticket. Michael was gearing up inside for battle, but was very unsure how it might go down. He was used to preparing in advance with surveillance, so there would be few surprises. Halfway to the island, he noticed a compound and asked the pilot what it was.

"The Muslims from Mandanao have a faction that believes in the jihad. Our government has been watching them, but has not had a reason to arrest anyone. It is advisable for Americans to stay away from this area of Cebu. It is even suggested that you take a bodyguard when traveling to Mandanao." The pilot stated emphatically.

"Nice to know," Michael said under his breath.

When the helicopter touched down, Michael thanked the pilot and asked how long he would be on the island.

"At thirteen hundred American dollars a trip, I imagine I'll be here for the day." The pilot said with a laugh.

"I might catch another ride today if things go well. Thanks." He told the pilot, then disembarked.

Resurrection   Philip N. Rogone

The first thing Michael noticed was that the island was like paradise, with lush foliage and beautiful flowers. The sand was a light yellow in color, and the water so clear that the sand was visible as the soft waves turned toward the shore. Beautiful island girls were walking along the beach in very tiny bikinis.

"This would be a great place to die." He thought to himself, unsure of his future.

Michael went to the front desk and waited while a Middle Eastern man was arranging to occupy two more family suites for a group that would be arriving later in the day. He overheard the man say the magic word "El Amin" and then watched as he departed. Michael told the front desk clerk he would take some time to look around before checking in and was encouraged to do so by the desk clerk. Michael left and followed the dark skinned man back to his suite. Michael walked around the suite and found it to be very quiet, almost too quiet. He decided to take a direct approach and kill everyone in the suite. He kept telling himself he had the element of surprise on his side. He put on a pair of latex gloves and tapped lightly on the door to the room. The man who had just entered opened the door and was met with a silenced shot to his head as blood sprayed behind the blast, which colored the beige tile floor with red spray, followed moments later by the man's body. Michael went from room to room and found the place totally deserted. He looked at the body of the man and decided to leave the occupants a message.

Michael pulled out his survival knife and made a crude incision into the dead man's abdomen. He exposed the small intestines and gently began to remove the jejunum. Michael knew that this would be between twenty-two and thirty-two feet long, which was more than enough for him to write a message on the floor. So in his best cursive writing, he wrote with the man's gut, "deathiscomingforyou."

Michael exited the way he came in, removed his latex gloves, and disposed of them on his way back to the heliport. The pilot was having a soda inside the tiny terminal when Michael approached.

"How about a ride back to Cebu?" He questioned with a smile.

The pilot nodded and dropped fifty pesos on the counter. The two men went to the helicopter and, in a matter of minutes, were up in the air.

Michael saw an approaching copter and commented to the pilot.

"Looks like today is a busy day for the resort."

"I'm surprised." The pilot remarked back to him.

Michael thought about the passengers of the approaching copter and wondered if they might be the recipients of his note. He thought about revisiting the resort when his company arrived. He reviewed the terrain and asked the pilot if he could land the copter on the hill above the peninsula resort.

"I can land this baby on a dime if you pay me enough." He assured his passenger.

"I'm John. What's yours?" Michael asked as he extended his hand.

"They call me Chopper." The pilot answered with a smile.

"Well, Chopper, what would you charge me for an entire day?" The Machine asked.

"Three thousand for the day plus the cost of fuel," Chopper remarked very nonchalantly.

Michael surprised the pilot when he told him that it would be fine. The two men joked with each other all the way back to the airport in Cebu. Michael liked the guy, and lately that wasn't happening too often.

The beeper vibrated on his waist. Michael looked down, then phoned the number.

"Ola Amigo!" The voice sang into the phone.

"Sorry you got brought into this shit." Michael was serious.

"Heard you might need a shadow," Xavier responded quietly.

"Where are you?" Michael asked.

"I'm in a private jet area near the heliport," Xavier said as he looked around.

"We should be at your location shortly. You ready to get busy?" Michael asked the old soldier.

"Yes," Xavier said flatly.

Michael turned to Chopper and told him they would be picking up a friend.

"Then I'll need you to take us back to Badian Island." He instructed the pilot.

"No problem, John," Chopper responded as he maneuvered the copter to land at the heliport circle.

Xavier Sanchez carried the tools of his trade to the door of the helicopter. When it opened, he was looking into the face of the Machine. He stared for just a moment, then handed his old friend his carry-on items.

"Shit, you sure got old!" Xavier said to Michael with a weathered grin as he entered the back seat.

"You don't look so bad yourself," Michael remarked, also with a smile.

The two men shook hands, then sat in silence as the copter moved through the beautiful blue sky. The thirty minutes went by quickly as the bird came down on the hill overlooking the Badian Resort. The two men got out and removed the bags. Michael put his head back in and told the pilot to pick them up when Michael called. He got a positive response as Michael handed him five thousand American dollars.

"See you later, John," Chopper yelled over the loud whirling blades of the craft and made a signal with his hands like he was talking to someone on the phone.

Zafeer was angry that Gabir had not come out to meet them at the heliport. This was an embarrassment to Zafeer. They took the golf cart shuttle to the Badian suites. Zafeer opened the door and called out for Gabir furiously. He almost tripped over the body of his subordinate upon entering. He stared at the gutted man's body and read the words displayed across the tiled floor. Zafeer became sick to his stomach and threw up violently upon seeing the disemboweled corpse. Nami stood motionless, he read the message made in guts, but refrained from showing any expression. However, he was feeling something he had not experienced in many years as his forehead began to perspire…it was fear. Weapons were drawn, and

Zafeer called out to the few soldiers who were still in their suites enjoying the amenities and the women. High alert came quickly as they realized they had been invaded.

Michael pointed to the Badian suites, where there was a lot of movement taking place. He explained to X. S. what they would be doing after nightfall in the beautiful resort. Three hours into their surveillance, Michael observed three SUVs arriving. Within minutes, the suites looked more like a fortress as guards were posted around each dwelling and weapons were at the ready.

Inside the suite, which had been cleaned up by his staff, Zafeer and Nami discussed their current situation and the San Francisco operation.

"Where are we in the operation?" Nami asked.

"The device was assembled at the compound and is being transported to the port of Cebu. It should be leaving tonight on the MV Oceanic Union, arriving in San Francisco harbor in about three weeks." Zafeer detailed.

"What information do we have about Mexico City, because it would appear the forces involved have found you again?" Nami inquired.

"We have information that an old FBI agent who was injured at the Pentagon may have assembled a group of mercenaries, but we believe that this is information the United States has released. It is more likely a Navy SEAL team sent by President Bush. So I have guards lined up along the beach area watching for infiltration from that approach. I also have a group of men watching for any approach from the hills behind us. Our location is actually safe due to limited access." Zafeer explained to his visiting superior.

"Why am I having trouble believing you, Zafeer?" Nami questioned his host and then added with assurance, "I do believe we have sufficient men to deal with a handful of their forces."

Nami was thinking of just when would be the right time to kill Zafeer. He concluded that early morning would be the best time, so he could depart by helicopter afterwards and still enjoy the rest of his day. He wanted a bit of entertainment from the local women, and Zafeer wanted to be sure his guest was taken care of well. So as the evening approached, things in the Badian suites began to become more relaxed, while outside their forces were on full alert. The leaders were feeling very good despite the terrible afternoon they had.

Michael the Machine and Xavier the Shadow were not talking all too much, but spent most of the afternoon positioning devices and setting up for a raid of monumental proportions. The Shadow had Tess provide the men with communication devices, four LAWs, ten grenades, and enough ammo to handle an Army company. Both men had equipped the weapons with silencers and would make every effort not to use the explosives unless absolutely necessary. X. S. also packed two sets of black and green fatigues for better camouflage. As the darkness began to take charge, the two soldiers darkened their faces with lampblack, a powder used for light-skinned soldiers in battle, and prepared to quietly blitzkrieg the Badian suites section of the beautiful resort.

The Machine started down the thickly vegetated jungle, moving in tune with the light breeze blowing against the foliage. Pinpointing the enemy was not difficult. The Machine knew his enemy very well, and most of this group had been trained in the deserts of the Middle East, not the jungle. He approached one of those that had been positioned toward their hilltop location. He waited and watched as his first victim took a final drag from his cigarette and looked down to stomp out the butt with his shoe. It would be the last thing he did as his mouth got covered and the survival knife sliced through his neck. The smoke that was expelled from his lungs only made it as far as the newly severed trachea, which assured the Machine his cut was deep enough. He lowered the remains slowly to the ground. Again, he moved forward, this time to the left until he reached his next target. His mind was only on the method of killing he would use to eliminate the enemy. This one was yawning, fatigued from hours of watch. He was put to sleep by the eight-inch blade as it was plunged into his heart.

There was no thought of Elizabeth or Tess as the knife made a gaping hole just above the vocal cords of victim number three. No arguments with God as victim number four found the fury of the Machine's blade, just the work of a master in the art of killing. When victim five's mouth was covered, he looked down and saw the blade disengage from his heart, blood pumping just a few more times out of reflex. The artist exterminated number six without a moment of conscience, no thought of whether the victim would be leaving a family behind, or a loved one, just the skill of a master craftsman doing what he did best.

The Machine continued to move left toward the suites. Unnoticed on the hill, his shadow with a night scope followed the Machine on his journey. Xavier had prepared himself for an all-out war, but had been trained well to be patient and not overreact. The best result was always to respond according to the situation, and the situation so far was in good hands.

Michael had removed the outermost perimeter defense on the hillside and made his way toward the beach area. This would be more difficult because there was far less natural concealment. He made his way near the water's edge and could see a soldier about every hundred yards from the small cabanas to the fire pits on the beach. The Machine moved in for the next kill, slow and methodical, raised his killing blade, and recollected the face of Alice's brother, who was the next victim. He lowered the blade and realized he needed to knock the kid out before he could move on. The Shadow on the hill had a limited view that far down near the huts, but could see a sentinel moving in Michael's direction. The sound of a long-range rifle's bullet moving through a human's heart makes a swooshing sound just before the body hits the ground. Honesto turned toward the sound when a hand went over his mouth, and a very quiet voice spoke quickly.

"Alice sent me here to get you. Do you understand?" The boy's head nodded, fear in his eyes.

The Machine couldn't take the chance that the boy would scream out or make an attempt to fight back once released, so he put pressure on the young neck until unconsciousness arrived, and then he slowly lowered Honesto to the ground and took the weapon from his limp arms. Michael knew that he needed to move faster and take out the enemy that would not be seen from his shadow's position. Xavier knew by the old soldier's movement that he would lose sight of him again. He turned his attention to the soldiers he could zero in on and began to fire rapidly from one target to the next, and within seven seconds, five more soldiers of the enemy were terminated. The Shadow was counting, and with twelve eliminated, there were still twenty-one left. Michael was counting too, and in just a few minutes their attack would be compromised not by anything they did but just by the nature of battle. All the other terrorists would be in very close proximity to the suites. Michael clicked his finger weapon into kill mode and pulled out his 380.

"This might get ugly soon." He thought to himself.

The door of the suite adjacent to where Michael left the message earlier opened casually, and a voice called out in Farsi. There was no response, so the man stepped out onto the raised porch and called out again. His body went limp as the Machine's silencer spat out two quick rounds into his head. That was all it took for things to get crazy, and Michael was on top of it. He moved back to a preordained position and pulled up an L.A.W. He knew he needed to be far enough away from his target to get the weapon to detonate, releasing fragments that would sear and burn even through metal. He needed to have at least one enemy remain alive long enough to stop the impending catastrophic attack on San Francisco. This weapon might do just that. He pulled back on the back chamber, activating it, pulled up the sight, and once the center of the suite was visible, he fired. In less than two seconds, the projectile exploded into incendiary fragments with a moment of blinding light as it destroyed the target's interior. As bodies exited the building, the high-powered rifle of the Shadow ensured they could not retaliate against the Machine. Michael was given a body count by his partner, another eight eradicated. He picked up another L.A.W. and let loose on the next suite, which produced similar results, and another six were counted out. Michael would have to get in close to kill the wounded who could still pose a threat. Michael could hear the swishing sound as his partner was still sending rounds just outside the other two rooms that had started to catch on fire as a result of the initial assault. He got another count, six more perished from the rifle. Seven more men were unaccounted for inside. He moved in, his 380 ready to end lives. Inside, he saw the devastation caused by the disposable rocket launcher. Four men near the door of the suite were reduced to smoldering flesh. Three to go as he continued toward the master bedroom, he could hear moaning and one man yelling at another. He kicked the door, moving to the ground, as gunfire followed. His 380 fired at a young well-dressed man with a thin beard that surrounded his face. Nami's weapon dropped as his shoulder exploded from Michael's revolver. In the corner of the room was Zafeer, bleeding from a leg wound and in no shape to pose a threat. The sound of pain he had heard was from another soldier who was immediately put out of his misery. Michael looked at both men cowering on the floor. He needed to make a tactical decision, which only took an instant, as he pointed the handgun at Nami and blew his head into hell with four rounds. He wanted Zafeer to see how brutal he could be, so that the information he needed would be more easily obtained. There would not be a lot of time. The resort security would be contacting the Cebu authorities to come as quickly as possible. Michael grabbed Zafeer and made his way back into the jungle, forcing the captured to walk despite his wounds. Michael contacted Chopper as they walked.

At the top of the hill, Michael found Xavier sipping whiskey from a metal flask. He smiled as the sniper handed him the container.

"Thanks. We don't have a lot of time." Michael said.

"Should we cut off his fingers first?" X.S. questioned as he watched the face of the terrorist, watching for a response.

"That might be a nice place to start," Michael responded almost lyrically.

"I need information, Zafeer." Michael continued.

"Who are you? What organization do you belong to?" Zafeer demanded to know. "You are not American military."

"I freelance killing insane jihadists and monsters with a mother complex," Michael said as he moved close to the terrorist.

Zafeer spat at the American. The Machine hit Zafeer hard against the side of his neck, which caused unconsciousness. The two soldiers grabbed their captive and their gear and headed for the clearing at the top of the hill, as the sound of helicopter blades reached their ears.

Once on board the craft and in the air, they looked down on the beautiful resort as flames consumed two of the Badian suites and resort staff were trying desperately to get it under control. X. S. pulled the whiskey flask out and offered the first sip to Michael, who accepted it.

"I am definitely too old for this shit," Michael said before he took a good swig.

"Maybe, but you sure are good at it," Xavier remarked.

Chapter Twenty: Cleaning Up

The helicopter was instructed to land near the Muslim compound. Michael had the flyer drop them off in the hills just north of the compound, about a mile or two. That would give them a tactical advantage. Chopper was curious but said nothing. Michael Xavier and their prisoner got out with their supplies, and Chopper was instructed to pick them up in the same location in six hours.

"If we aren't here within five minutes of your landing, then go home and forget you ever saw us. Understood?" Michael instructed.

"Got it, John. Good luck." Chopper said before leaving.

Once on the ground, Michael got extremely different. The cold, hard look of death was facing Zafeer El Amin, and the man trembled. Michael took out his hunting knife and began to sharpen it with a honing stone. He stared at his enemy but said nothing. Xavier knew to get away from the Machine. After about five minutes and testing the blade for sharpness, he moved closer to his enemy.

"I am going to kill you, that much is for sure, but how I kill you will be up to you. Understand?" He questioned Zafeer. The man nodded in the affirmative.

"I need to know if there is a bomb heading for San Francisco Bay. I need all the information: the name of the ship, expected arrival date, and if there are crazed jihadists aboard, and if so, how many." The Machine informed without the hint of emotion. Zafeer began speaking almost immediately. He wanted to die quickly. He gave his captor all that he requested and more.

"I am a tool for the king of Saudi Arabia, who is working with Iran leadership to expel the American intervention in the Middle East. There is a spy for our country who has infiltrated the United States Senate, but I do not know his name. This is all the information I have…I swear to Allah." Michael was true to his word. He put the knife back into his military sheath, pulled out the 380 silencer attached, and gave the terrorist a third eye right in the middle of his forehead. Zafeer slumped backward and died. Xavier came from the bushes and asked his partner.

"What's next?"

"Next, we go into this training center and kill every last one of them. All must perish, or the war lingers eventually into the hands of politicians who will fuck it up completely. This needs to be done our way." Michael said with authority.

The two men moved out, leaving the carcass. They were ready for action in no time at all, and once the Shadow moved into a position where he had a view of most of the camp, the Machine moved in for the close kills. With silencers in place, the two men began killing. First, picking those men that were alone or in groups of two, then moving closer to the camp where some were training. This somewhat silent attack went on for almost two hours. The Shadow was practicing his long-range kills on unsuspecting targets, while the Machine was slicing through tissue for artery access and dropping men easily with the 380 revolver. The zealots didn't put up much of a fight, and the ninety-three men who had decreed their dedication to killing Americans anywhere were sent to the God of Abraham unfulfilled. Michael went through the compound, finding a cache of money, pesos, and mostly American hundred-dollar bills.

217

He thought to himself, "I love the way these nice terrorists keep leaving me lots of money."

He found some food in their mess tent and brought it to his partner. While they waited for their ride, the two old soldiers ate and talked about what they had been doing for the past thirty years. Michael told him about Elizabeth and how he got into the messy business of killing again.

Anymore blackouts?" Xavier asked.

"Not that I know of. So what about you?" Michael asked.

Xavier started with his return to America after serving for his country. He told Michael he had arrived in San Antonio, greeted by hippies protesting his existence and describing him as a baby killer. After he was released for assault with intent to kill, a charge that was later dropped, he went home and started working with his father detailing cars. He told his old friend that he had wanted to refurbish old cars and eventually took over his dad's business and began to do just that. He made a lot of money renovating classic Chevrolets and Fords, for egocentric college kids who were happy spending their daddy's money. Xavier had actually made over a million dollars in his classic car business, which gave him too much free time, and that caused him to drink too much.

"I got into a fight with a Marine when Lamia brought me to D.C. So what's the story with her?" He asked Michael.

"She's a hell of a gal, but I'm afraid before too long she will only be hurt or worse get into trouble for helping me," Michael admitted.

Before long, the helicopter showed up. The pilot got out of the aircraft and helped the men load up. He turned to Michael and said.

218

"A picture that looks kinda like you has been posted at the terminal. I think I need to get you out of this area."

"Any suggestions?" Michael asked.

"I could take you to Francisco Bangoy International Airport, it's about two hundred and seventy-four km, and that would mean we make it on fumes, but at least it's far enough away that they wouldn't be looking for you there." Chopper strongly suggested.

"Sounds like a good idea." Xavier chirped in.

"Okay," Michael said, nodding his approval of the idea.

The experienced pilot really knew how to get the most out of his aircraft, and the helicopter landed with the fuel gauge just above empty. The two-hour trip at high speed, going with the wind, didn't hurt. Michael paid his pilot over seven thousand dollars, and the two men shook hands while Xavier was pulling the equipment out of the back seat.

"Leave it all. None of this can go with us." Michael said to his partner.

"Chopper, can you store this for me in case I need it one day?" Michael asked the man he had come to like.

"Just call me, and it will be at your disposal," Chopper assured him.

"One more thing, I was told there was a man named Aqeel here in the Philippines who might have something to do with the bad guys. If you hear anything, could you give me a call?"

"Consider it done, John," Chopper assured him.

They shook again and said goodbye. The two tired soldiers made their way to the terminal to catch a flight anywhere away from the Philippines. They looked at each other and smiled when the only international flights were going to Singapore and Malaysia.

"I think we're going for some R and R, soldier," Michael said to his old friend.

"And on their dime...I love it." X. S. finished the thought.

"I had better get in touch with Tess to give her the ship intelligence."

Michael reached into his pocket and dialed her cell. It rang just once when she picked up. He was glad to hear her voice one more time.

"Hi. I have information about the attempt to blow up San Francisco. However, the way that the city has become a modern-day Sodom, you don't have to do anything with the information if you don't want to." He said jokingly.

"Understood, but it would be another expensive mess we would have to clean up, so go ahead, please." She joked back at him.

Michael spent the next ten minutes detailing his actions in the Philippines. He gave her the name of the ship and told Tess to be very careful because there was a traitor in the Senate, and to watch herself. He filled her in on the attack on the terrorist compound, but refrained from too much detail. Then he told her that Zafeer had been eliminated and where the body could be found.

"I don't want any credit for something I didn't do, but expect the effort to bring me in to intensify. They have a better description of me, and it will be on the wire if it hasn't arrived already." He told her.

"Oh, it arrived a few hours ago, but the sketch has you with a beard and no moustache. Still looks pretty handsome to me." She said, softening her tone.

"Don't get me started, you're too far away to touch." He said.

"Where are you and Xavier now?" She asked.

"We'll be in Singapore. I'll send the Shadow back to San Antonio in a few days." He told her.

"What about you? Where will you go?" She asked.

"For now, I'm here, the news will go out about the brutality of the deaths I caused, and those horrible details will fester within the enemy, and I'll be around in the darkness. Wherever they pop up, I'll be there, and I'll make them feel the threat of me somewhere in the night, and they'll make mistakes or be too cautious, and I will exploit that weakness. The people of our country have been fed a bunch of bullshit about what has made America the greatest country in the world. It isn't our goodness or openness. It is our resolve to fight the enemy for our self-preservation until every last one of them is dead and forgotten. That's our strength. When the evil in the world learn to fear us again, it will be safer, but for now, a lesson needs to be learned, and it would appear I'm the teacher. When I was a kid in the jungles of Viet Nam, they called me the Machine because I killed without emotion. I became the most vicious killer I could be, but I didn't ever think I was fighting to keep America safe. It was someplace far away, unemotional, a job. 9/11 brought the reason to fight and kill to a much more personal place. This is my country, and anyone who tries to hurt it is going to die, and they will die badly." Michael said, pouring out his soul.

Epilogue: The Start of the Personal War

Tess hung up the phone just as Ted Hobson came through her door. He introduced himself. She was still reeling from the phone call and the words Michael expressed so sincerely. She was caught off guard when Ted asked if they could talk candidly.

"I know you were expecting to get the position I have, and for that I'm sorry. Chet apparently made up his mind about a replacement for your boss long before he even left. I'm hoping we can work together as a team. The fact that Chet promoted you to liaison between the FBI and the CIA is a testament to his respect for you."

"Thanks, Ted. I appreciate you coming in here like this. It's something my old boss would have done, and we worked very well together for a very long time." She responded, feeling better about her new boss.

Ted was a good-looking man in his mid-forties, with very short hair still in a military style, a squared-off jaw, very white teeth, great blue eyes, and a warm smile. Tess couldn't help but like the guy. He had made their introduction heartfelt and sincere.

"Speaking about your old boss, I need you to brief me on Michael Angelino."

"I don't think it's him doing these killings, if that's what you're getting at. He has always been a kind religious man." She lied, trying to keep Michael's involvement in question.

"Tess, I've read the file. Michael Angelino was a trained killer and one of the best to come out of Viet Nam. Whatever happened to him on 9/11 has resurrected what he once was. I'll be honest with you, Tess; I believe this guy is probably acting alone. Now I agree he may have gone off the deep end, but nonetheless, he has done a number on the enemy. The son of a bitch has become my hero in less than three weeks." Ted Hobson said, truly excited.

"If Michael has done any of this, he needs medical help. He may have had a split in his personality. He was having severe blackouts after the accident." She went on to defend her old boss.

"I know that you have feelings for the old guy. Chet told me that you were pretty broken up about him leaving, but Tess, you need to review the file again. Michael was like a serial killer with a license in Viet Nam." Ted continued. "I think he just hit again in the Philippines."

"What?" She pretended to be in total disbelief.

"We have a preliminary count of somewhere in the neighborhood of a hundred and thirty bodies, and they said there may be more. Tess, who else could kill like that? We don't have a secret group out there killing people, Bush would be on trial if the Democrats thought for a minute he had anything to do with this?" Hobson tried to convince her.

"Okay, let's just say for the moment you're right. What do we do?" She asked, trying to get some insight into his train of thought.

"Nothing," Ted stated emphatically.

"Nothing?" Tess questioned.

"Right, absolutely nothing. Our office will, however, be leaking out information that might be of let's say some assistance to a killing force of one." Ted Hobson confessed his motives.

"We can't do that. We need to get the guy some help." Tess went on. "Anyway, there's no way he could be capable of all this."

"I spent my whole military career doing it by the book. What I have seen since I retired is an enemy that wants to hurt innocent women and children and takes pride in doing so. They are without honor, and they deserve whatever happens to them."

The news report from Al Jazeera of the slaughter in the Philippines made King Abdullah fly into a rage. His advisors were fearful about what this news might mean. Would these unknown forces now turn their attention toward their country? Who could be capable of such horrible devastation with no evidence left behind? Their fears were brought up in their council meeting with the king, who began dialing as his advisors tried to make some sense of this retribution.

The room got silent as the king spoke into the phone. They watched as he spoke affirmatively and then hung up. He looked around the room and told all but one of his advisors to leave. Sirhan Ramadan leaned closer to the king after the room cleared.

"Aqeel has indicated that it is time to activate the English and American brothers of Allah. Let us see how they handle destruction from within."